COUSIN KATE

"You said your cousin was shy and lonely, and we were supposed to be nice to her," accused Miranda.

"It's not my fault the boys like her," I said, but no one seemed to believe me.

"She's your responsibility," said Jennifer. "You invited her in with the gang."

Suddenly I was furious. "What am I supposed to do?" I yelled.

Jennifer didn't answer. She also didn't speak to me. Neither did Miranda.

The others kids stomped off in angry groups of twos while I brooded over how fragile my terrific senior year was and wondered how long the other girls would be mad at me.

Other Avon Flare Books by
Nancy J. Hopper

CARRIE'S GAMES
THE TRUTH OR DARE TRAP

Avon Camelot Books
APE EARS AND BEAKY

RIVALS

Nancy J. Hopper

AN AVON FLARE BOOK

AVON BOOKS
A division of
The Hearst Corporation
105 Madison Avenue
New York, New York 10016

The Lodestar Books edition contains the following Library of Congress Cataloging
in Publication Data:

Hopper, Nancy J.
  Rivals.

  "Lodestar books."
  Summary: Joni sees her senior year in high school falling apart when her
gorgeous cousin comes to live with her and starts moving in on her life,
including her boyfriend.
  [1. Cousins—Fiction] I. Title.
PZ7.H7792Ri   1985   [Fic]   85-13108

First Flare Printing: December 1987

FLARE TRADEMARK REG. U.S. PAT. OFF. AND IN OTHER COUNTRIES, MARCA
REGISTRADA, HECHO EN U.S.A.

Printed in the U.S.A.

K-R 10 9 8 7 6 5 4 3 2

to my parents
Joyce B. and David L. Swartz

1

The minute cousin Kate walked off the plane, I knew we could never be friends. I stared at her and hoped for some mistake, but even then I realized there was none. The only other passengers to disembark were two middle-aged men, a college guy carrying a guitar, and an ancient woman clutching a cane in her left hand and the portable-stair railing with her right.

The college student paused on the tarmac and turned toward my cousin, stopping her for several seconds. Kate reached up to push a strand of hair from one cheek, then laughed.

I couldn't hear the laugh. I must have been a hundred yards away, standing with my parents behind a wall of plate glass. Besides, I was still trying to adjust to the fact that my alarm had gone off at 6:00 A.M. the morning after the Homecoming Dance.

I had stumbled out of bed and grabbed a pair of jeans from the pile on my floor and a rumpled top from the back of a chair. I thought I'd combed my hair, but I wasn't certain. There wasn't time for anything else, not if we were going to make the airport by seven thirty.

Naturally the plane was an hour late. Naturally one food-vending machine was out of order, and the other was empty. I huddled in a seat in the passengers' lounge and hovered between sleep and consciousness, my mind straying back over what I remembered of Kate.

It wasn't much. Although they'd lived near us when we girls were little, Uncle Raymond had gotten a job in Berkeley at the University of California when Kate was five. The following year her mother died, and her father hadn't brought Kate east for a visit since.

Uncle Raymond is a herpetologist. I used to think that meant he studied diseases, but Mother once explained that a herpetologist specializes in snakes. I don't know why anyone would want to do that, but my uncle did.

When Mother first told me Kate was coming to live with us for five months, she said that Uncle Raymond had been given money by the United States government to go to Africa to study snakes. He couldn't take Kate with him because he would be traveling around a lot and it would be hot and full of germs and maybe revolutions, plus very expensive for the plane tickets. Besides, he wanted her to finish her senior year in high school on schedule.

"Raymond made arrangements for Kate to stay with friends in Oakland, but the friends were transferred to Chicago and aren't settled in yet," Mom told me. "So she's coming here to us. Oh, Joni, isn't it wonderful! I've always wished you two could get to know each other."

I must admit I was pretty glad too. "We can get a second bed for my room," I offered. "Or she can have my bed, and I'll sleep on a cot." We could stay up late nights, whispering and giggling. It would be a five-month slumber party.

"I'll straighten my room," I added recklessly. "I'll throw things out, hang up my clothes, put all my records back in their jackets."

Mom raised her eyebrows. They are black and furry and used to be one line before she began plucking them in the middle. Mom and I look a lot alike, but I have never needed to pluck my eyebrows.

I offered the ultimate enticement. "I'll clean under my bed," I said. I have been avoiding that chore since some time during my junior year.

"She can have Doug's room. You can help me do it over."

"But what about Doug?" I still had hopes of Kate's bunking with me.

"He'll hardly be home while she's here. Kate is going to Chicago over Thanksgiving, and Doug will be here only two weeks at Christmas. He can sleep on the daybed in the family room."

"But Mom—"

"We want to be kind. Sleeping in your room would be guest abuse."

Since I wanted Kate to be happy, I helped Mother move Doug's stuff to the attic, pick out new curtains and a spread, and hang a Degas print of dancers on the wall opposite the bed. Then I mostly got on with my life.

During those weeks when I thought of my cousin at all, I thought of her as small and sort of anemic-looking, shy with big glasses and stringy, neutral-looking hair. At least she'd had big glasses and stringy hair in the photographs I'd seen of her. Nevertheless, I was certain it would be easy to fit her into my gang. They were warm and friendly kids who would naturally go out of their way for a lost and lonely stranger, a semi-orphan.

Now, watching Kate cross to the doors of the terminal, I wasn't certain. She didn't look the slightest bit lost or lonely. She was talking with the college boy and not even looking around for us to meet her. She looked as if she had hopped planes from California to Ohio every week of her entire life.

Suddenly I regretted grabbing the first coat I got in my hands when we left the house that morning. It was an old khaki raincoat Doug had bought in an army surplus store and left behind when he went to college.

Wrapping the coat around me more closely, I followed my parents to the reception area. I yawned and rubbed at my face while we waited for Kate to come up the escalator, but I was no longer sleepy. It was more of a nervous yawn. I could see Kate clearly, behind the old lady with the cane and in front of the boy.

My cousin was tall and cool-looking, slender and graceful. Everything about her seemed long: long legs, long hands, hair to her shoulders. And that hair. It wasn't the slightest bit neutral or stringy. It was a beautiful muted red with golden highlights, silky in appearance even at a distance. She didn't wear glasses either. As she came closer, I could see her eyes were greenish blue. They matched the blazer and skirt she wore with tan leather shoes and purse.

"Kathleen," Mother said, and gathered my cousin into her arms in a big hug.

I shoved my hands deep into my raincoat pockets and tried to remember if I'd combed my hair and whether I was wearing my good jeans or the pair with a hole worn in the seat.

"You are exactly like your mother—beautiful," said Mom, and she started to cry.

Kate seemed unmoved. She was probably used to being called beautiful. Me, people call attractive—except for Jason, and he's biased.

"You must be—" Kate hesitated, glancing at me.

"Joni," I said. "Hi, Kathy."

Kate turned toward my dad and let him hug her, her cheeks flushing pink, then went with my parents to the baggage counter. As I trailed after them, I wondered if it had been a deliberate plot on Uncle Raymond's part to make his daughter look toady in photographs.

Kate's three suitcases matched her purse and her shoes. I figured they would. My entire luggage consisted of a small nylon cosmetics case and a duffel bag.

Kate didn't seem satisfied with the luggage handed her. "I had a box," she said, "square, with a carrying handle."

I dragged myself out of bed at 6:00 A.M. and this girl didn't even care. All she was interested in was some stupid box.

"Miss," said a male voice from behind my left shoulder. "You were concerned about this, so I brought it up myself."

"Oh, thank you," said Kate.

The man in the blue uniform seemed amply rewarded by the flash of her smile and the warm expression in the green eyes. He touched his hat and was on his way before Dad could tip him.

"What's that?" asked Mom, eyeing the box Kate was holding. It wasn't very large, but it was sturdily built and it had small air holes in the top. There were two latches. A faint rustling came from within.

"It's Alfred," said Kate with another dazzling smile. "My pet snake."

I almost threw up. I mean, I have had gerbils and mice and even a hamster once, but a snake? No way. My empty stomach gave a lurch at the thought of it.

Mom was unshaken. Since she teaches first grade, she is used to most of the peculiarities of human behavior. I did notice that Dad put Alfred in the trunk along with the other luggage, instead of taking him into the car with us.

I only said one thing on the way home. "How do you know Alfred is a he?" I asked.

Kate glanced at me and wet her red lips. "I don't know for sure," she admitted. "I guessed."

Oh, fine, I thought. So Alfred lays eggs or whatever snakes do, and suddenly our home is like the reptile house at the zoo.

"You have Doug's room," I said when we pulled up in front of our house. I had to say something. Mom had noticed my silence and was giving me meaningful looks.

"Why don't you show her, Joni," said Mother. "I'll see about lunch, and your father can track down the aquarium you used for your gerbil."

"For Alfred," said Dad with a small shudder. I didn't know if the shudder was real or pretend. I took the two biggest suitcases and let my cousin carry the other one and the box with the air holes.

It was too early to be preparing lunch, I realized as I trudged up the stairs in my khaki coat, bearing suitcases like a porter. My mother wanted my cousin and me to get acquainted, to start exchanging girlish secrets and giggling together.

"That's my parents' room," I said on the way down the hall.

Kate ignored me. She was staring into my room

opposite. I had been going to clean it, but I hadn't had time. There were two pairs of jeans on the floor, the bed was unmade, cosmetics and magazines and records were strewn all over the place. It was in pretty good shape for me.

"This is your room," I said loudly from the end of the hall. I walked in and set the cases down at the foot of the bed.

Kate followed me. She didn't look at the Degas reproduction or the new spread and curtains or anything else in the room. She went straight to the double windows that opened onto our small front yard and the street.

Outside the windows, the limbs of our big old maple arched high above the house, its leaves glowing bright yellow, making a golden awning between the windows and the sky.

"That's fantastic," said Kate.

"The sugar maple two doors down is even better. It's red."

"Leaves don't turn color in the part of California where I live."

"I know. Mom told me." I waited, and finally she turned to survey the room.

"What a big space," she said. Her eyes roamed over the furniture, across the Degas dancers. "The ceilings are so high. I feel almost as if I'm outside."

I must have looked puzzled, because she added, "We don't have a whole lot of old houses in California."

I guessed it was a compliment. I didn't get a chance to find out, because my father and mother both arrived, bearing the ten-gallon tank, the screen that served as a lid, and the big rock we'd used to weigh the screen down and prevent my gerbil from escaping.

"Where do you want this?" Dad asked Kate.

"On the desk. I can arrange things later." Kate put the carrying box down next to the aquarium, opened the latches, and slowly raised the lid.

There was a long deliberate hiss, then a violent vibration.

"Shut up, Alfred," said Kate. She reached into the box, caught the creature behind the head, and lifted him. His long body dangled limp from her right hand. She put her left hand under him and carefully lowered him into the tank.

Alfred flipped on his back for about thirty seconds and lay absolutely still. Then he turned over onto his stomach again and coiled quietly behind the glass, as if he weren't quite certain whether to bite or to hide.

"How interesting!" said my mother.

He was sort of interesting—for a snake. He had grayish sides covered by big black spots and a narrow head with a funny little snout on the end of his nose. He also had his mouth shut so I couldn't see his fangs.

"What does Alfred eat?" asked Dad.

"Eggs sometimes," said Kate. "A live toad now and then." She picked up the rock. "I'm glad you thought of this." She put it in the cage beside Alfred.

"It goes on top," said Dad. "To hold down the screen."

"Oh, okay." As she recovered the rock and put it on top of the screen, a faint smile crossed Kate's lips.

After making more noise over Alfred and how happy we all were that my cousin was spending the next five months with us, Mother said she had more work to do in the kitchen, and Dad said he was going out to pick up the *Times* at the drugstore.

"You help Kate," Mother told me on the way out the door.

Kate and I eyed each other like two strange dogs meeting for the first time. She glanced away first, her eyes flicking toward the windows.

"Is there anything I can do, Kathy?" I asked. Maybe she was hungry or wanted an extra blanket. It was warm in California.

"To start with, you can call me *Kate*."

"All right." That was going to be difficult. Somehow, *Kathy* sounded warmer and more familiar, more like the friends I wanted us to be.

As Kate put her biggest suitcase on the bed and opened it, I went to the closet to check for hangers. Then I watched her take clothes from the case and put them on the hangers. Her hands were shaking a little. She probably was nervous.

So I wouldn't seem to be staring at her, I went to look in the tank at Alfred. He wasn't doing anything. I tapped lightly on the glass with one finger. He raised his head, staring at me, and gave a ceremonial hiss. His little forked tongue flicked out. I thought I remembered reading somewhere that snakes smelled with their tongues, but I wasn't certain.

"Kathy—" It just slipped out.

"The name is *Kate!*" The golden red hair swung as she jerked her head up, and the green eyes sparkled angrily.

"Sorry," I gulped. "I forgot."

"Well, don't."

We stared at each other across the room. Then Kate put one hand to her forehead and held it. "I'm sorry," she said. "I didn't mean to snap. It's just that—" She stopped, dropped her hand, and looked back at her open suitcase. "I guess I'm sort of tired."

"That's okay," I said. That's me, Joni Allen, always trying to be agreeable, the good sport. "I have homework to do. I'll see you later."

Downstairs I sat at the kitchen table, stared at my homework in German, and listened to Mom ask questions about the Homecoming Dance.

"Didn't you have a good time?" she asked after all my short answers.

"Sure," I said. "I just don't feel like talking about it."

Mom sighed. Then she said, "I think it's really great that Jennifer's parents are giving that party Saturday night to introduce Kate to your friends. Jennifer's mother called yesterday and said she'd reserved the log cabin at Silver Park."

I grunted.

"She invited your dad and me, but I told her we had a prior commitment."

I didn't say anything.

Mom frowned in exasperation. "What's the matter?" she asked. "Cat got your tongue?"

"No," I said. "Not really." To myself I added, Kate got my tongue.

2

I didn't realize it, but as I sat at the kitchen table that morning, my senior year was already divided in two parts: Before Kate and After Kate. The After Kate part had begun when my cousin stepped off that plane. As for Before Kate, I don't know anything that could have been more like my life as I wanted it than the night of the Homecoming Dance. For long weeks after her arrival, I would classify that evening in my mind as The Last Good Time in the Life of Joni Allen.

It was a good time from the moment I finished dressing in my bedroom and stared into the mirror over my dresser. If I threw my eyes out of focus so I looked quite blurred, I could pass for gorgeous. Unfortunately, my eyes quickly returned to normal and so did the girl in the mirror. I eyed her critically.

My two best assets—actually my only assets—my thick dark hair and large eyes exactly matched the deep brown satin of my dress. I had shampooed my hair that morning, and it shone. The smooth, blunt cut came right below my ears, falling forward to screen my face when I bent my head.

My skin, which is so fair I get instant sunburn at the pool, looked white and delicate against my smoothly fitting gown. I leaned toward the mirror and made my eyes go soft and seductive.

At that moment I smiled, and the image fell apart. I have a standard nose, nothing too noticeable, but my mouth is wide, and I have absolutely huge teeth.

'Joni,'' Mother called up the stairs. ''Jason is here.''

Jason. My gaze moved to the music box he had given me for Christmas our sophomore year, and I reached to pick it up. When I turned the small golden key on the base, a tinkling tune spilled out into my room, the notes liquid but distinct. As I had a thousand times, I hummed to the music while I watched the tiny figures dancing on the top.

The boy was tall like Jason; the girl, a brunette like me. They spun to the music, the girl looking up at her partner, her head tilted, a smile curving her lips.

''Joni!'' Mom yelled.

I put the music box back in its place, gave one last quick glance in the mirror, and swept down the stairs and into our living room. On the bottom step I hesitated so that Jason could see me at my best.

Jason is handsome, tall and blond, with blue eyes, a straight nose, and a perfect mouth. He is almost a year older than a lot of the kids in our class, popular and smart, and everything a girl could want.

I think I love him, but I'm not sure.

''Stand in front of the fireplace so I can take your picture,'' said my dad.

Grabbing me by one hand, Jason pulled me with

him to the fireplace. He slipped one arm around my waist and hugged me tight to his side.

"Look happy," instructed my father, crouching behind the camera he had mounted on a tripod.

Dad is a camera nut. He documents every single event that ever happens in our family, and lots of those events have included Jason. There are pictures of Jason and me before the prom last spring, Jason and me together on a horse at the county fair, and even a picture of Jason kissing me on the cheek at my third birthday party. I had decided if we didn't end up married to each other, our family album was going to look very embarrassing.

"Have fun at the dance," said Dad, swatting me on the butt as I passed him on the way to the door.

He didn't need to tell me that. Anytime our gang was together, we had fun, and we were all at the dance—from Jennifer and Sam, who like Jason and me had gone steady for years, to Miranda and Harry, who had been dating for only a month. Amy Bole, my best friend, met Jason and me at the edge of the dance floor, her eyes sparkling with excitement.

"Isn't it terrific?" she said, leaning back slightly to look up at us. Amy can't be more than five feet tall and weighs less than one hundred pounds. With her carrot-colored hair upswept, in her high heels and green dress, she looked like a life-sized doll.

Her date for Homecoming was James Shoji Tomimoto, or Tomo as everybody calls him. Tomo's American, born in this country of parents from Tokyo. He's muscular and very well built, but he is only two inches taller than Amy in her heels. Standing beside them, Jason and I towered like a couple of giants.

Jennifer and Sam came to join us, but I barely had time to say hello before Jason pulled me away onto the dance floor. I figured we'd see them later, at intermission, but instead I found myself standing alone with Jason, watching the queen and her attendants and their dates on the bandstand. I looked at the younger girls and tried to pick out who would be next year's Homecoming queen.

"I wonder where we'll be next year," I said to Jason.

"College." He made the word sound exciting, but a feeling like a cold draft passed over me, and I rubbed at my bare arms. What could be better than now?

Of all the seniors that night, the kids in our gang were among the luckiest. When the dance was over, it was as if our evening was only beginning. We piled into two cars and drove to Akron, to The Bank, which is just about the best restaurant around. Everybody had wanted to go there, but Amy and I had planned early and made our reservations in September.

The eight of us were shown directly to the table, large and round with a snowy white cloth. It was in the main room of the restaurant, next to a marble column, in what used to be the lobby of the First National Bank and Trust.

Our marble column was one of six, thick and fluted, rising in stony splendor to the ceiling of the second floor. Across the room by another column, I could see Marcy and a group of her friends, Jamie and Elaine and some boys. Steve Pellosi saw me looking and waved. I waved back, then stared around the huge space we were in.

In the center of the room beneath the enormously high ceiling hung a large chandelier, made of hundreds of glass beads and drops. The walls were covered with flocked red paper, and the tables glistened with glass and silver.

"I wonder if they still arrange loans," said Jason. "I have the feeling I'm going to need one."

"I'll go halves on a glass of water," I offered. "Or fruit." I nodded at the cornucopia of fruit in the center of our table.

"I think that's just the centerpiece," said Jason.

A waiter in a little red coat and a ruffled white shirt came to take our order, then went away and came back again. Another man filled our glasses with water, and a waitress took our beverage order. By that time the band had come back from a break, and Jason wanted to dance.

I don't remember dinner. I do know I loved the dessert cart and could have eaten everything on it. I settled for Baked Alaska, a super dessert with cake and ice cream on the inside, covered with meringue and baked. Then I ate part of Jason's coconut pie and tasted the German torte Amy ordered. Feeling a new sophisticated me, I ordered coffee to follow dessert.

"You don't drink coffee," said Jason.

"Now I do." I sipped cautiously. The coffee tasted hot and bitter on my tongue. I pretended to sip again, and looked wide-eyed at Jason over the pale rim of delicate china. Tonight I was discovering new depths in myself, new pleasures. I reached languidly to the centerpiece and broke a single green grape from its stem. I held it between my fingers for a long moment, then placed it slowly between my lips.

The grape was plastic.

It was amazingly difficult to keep a tender, warm, sophisticated expression on my face while trying to decide what to do with a plastic grape in my mouth. I shifted it with my tongue, trying not to crunch down and break a tooth. Perhaps I could chew and swallow it like some huge repulsive pill, or maybe I could secretly spit it into my napkin.

Maybe the grape was covered with a poisonous paint, and already I was doomed to a painful death. Hoping it was harmless and would dissolve easily in my stomach acid, I rolled the grape indecisively against my molars.

"Why don't you just spit it out," suggested Jason. "They probably charge extra if you eat the center-piece."

"What I like best about you is your natural-born ability to lead, to make decisions," I told him when I had removed the grape from my mouth and balanced it on the rim of my coffee saucer.

Jennifer, who sat opposite me, noticed and looked puzzled.

"They aren't ripe yet," I explained.

"Do you want to dance again?" asked Jason. "Or should I order you another dinner?"

Of course I wanted to dance. That was what I was there for, wasn't it? To eat and laugh and talk and dance, to have a good time. I took Jason's hand and went with him to the dance floor. I should have been tired and sleepy and so stuffed with food I could barely move, but I wasn't. I wanted to be like the couple on the music box; I wanted the tune to play forever, and Jason to move me around the dance floor. I wanted to be secure and happy in his arms, forever.

Every part of my life seemed right: Jason, school, my friends, my family. I was having a terrific senior year. That was the way it was for me—until Kate came to stay with us and changed everything.

3

Although she had already seen Kate's counselor to set up her schedule, Mom offered to drive us to school Monday morning. She and my cousin were to stop by the counselor's office first thing, so that Kate would feel more at home and confident.

Although I had no doubts about Kate's confidence, I wasn't about to turn down a free ride to school. I offered to run upstairs and get Kate when the time came to leave and she hadn't appeared.

Her door was closed. I tapped on it, then rapped loudly. Kate threw it open.

"Mom's ready," I said.

"Just a second."

Her room reeked of strong perfume. I held my breath and stood in the doorway, watching Kate as she sprayed herself one more time and then directed the atomizer around the room.

"Agh," I muttered when I could hold my breath no longer. "What is that stuff?"

"Tempestuous."

"It smells like a funeral in here."

"Anything to kill the stink." Kate aimed a long fusillade toward the aquarium on the desk and then put the atomizer down on her dresser. She picked up a comb and ran it through her hair.

"What stink?" My eyes were beginning to water, and my nose itched.

"Him." Kate nodded over her shoulder at Alfred. He didn't move or anything, but I thought he seemed depressed. "Can you imagine going out on a date and the guy telling you you smelled like a copperhead?"

"That happened?"

"No," she said gloomily, "but I figure it's only a matter of time."

At that moment I felt closer to Kate than at any time since she'd arrived. Unfortunately, as she put down the comb, she looked at me and asked, "You're wearing *that?*"

That was my new red plaid skirt and a genuine part-angora sweater. Kate was wearing jeans and a tunic top. The top looked as if it might have been designed for Brooke Shields.

"Just a little something I found on the floor of my closet," I told her.

"Girls!" yelled Mom from the bottom of the stairs. "Girls, you are going to be late for school."

"I care," I muttered as I followed Kate. We left Alfred looking downcast and smelling of Tempestuous. Personally, I preferred the snake's odor. It might not be flowery, but at least it didn't make my eyes red and my nose run.

Mother didn't say a thing about Kate's perfume, but I did notice she rolled down the window on the driver's side before we had gone two blocks. I was trapped between the two of them and had little fresh air until we separated at the school.

The only class Kate and I had together was third-period Health, a freshman course. I'd asked Kate what she was doing in Health her senior year, but she'd evaded the question. Had she been the victim of numerous schedule foul-ups the way I had, or was there another reason?

Next to Computers II, Health was my least favorite subject. I had elected Computers II so that I could study computers in college and be guaranteed a good job later; but Health was required for graduation from high school. The big difference between them was that I was pulling an A in Health, although I didn't like the teacher.

Mrs. Mastriani seems to have an idea that if she is the slightest bit nice to us students, we will take advantage of her and run completely out of control. She is thin and dark and mean, and wears braces even though she must be forty. She also looks as if she has a headache most of the time.

"People," said Mrs. Mastriani as I came into the room. "People, take your seats and please be quiet." She says the same thing every single day. The students are slow to listen to her, partly because she acts as if we won't. Besides, she always says this before the bell rings. Who's going to sit down and shut up before then?

When we were finally in our seats and almost quiet, Mrs. Mastriani picked up her health book to glance at it. Then she put it down again. I knew from having read the chapter that we were to begin studying human anatomy and reproduction. Leave it to the school system to assign someone like Mrs. Mastriani to teach freshmen the difference between boys and girls. They probably know more about it than she does.

"I suppose——" she lisped. The braces sometimes caused that.

The door opened and Kate came in, holding an admit slip. She had probably gotten lost on her way from another class. She hesitated, then crossed the front of the room and held the slip out toward Mrs. Mastriani.

"Beauty and the beast," said the boy behind me. He wasn't very loud, but loud enough for most everyone to hear.

"I'm supposed to be in here this period, Ms. Mastriani," said Kate in a low voice.

"Miz?" said Mrs. Mastriani, then more loudly, "Miz?" She snorted through her nose. "It is *Mrs.* Mastriani."

"Yes, sir—er—ma'am." Kate gulped and turned bright red. Everyone in the class laughed, and some guy in the back hooted.

Mrs. Mastriani took the slip and told Kate to sit in the fourth row in the empty seat next to the windows, right beside me. I lowered my eyes to my book as she came down the aisle, hoping Mrs. Mastriani didn't know that Kate and I were cousins and that Kate was living with me.

Mrs. Mastriani pulled down a chart like a map in front of the chalkboard. Instead of continents and oceans, it contained two transparent figures: male and female.

There was a sound like sighing in the room, and I had a sudden surge of sympathy for Mrs. Mastriani. Teaching Health to freshmen must be a lot like trying to sell bikinis to Eskimos.

She must have thought so too. She turned to us and said, "Now, people, before we start studying the body systems, I want to tell you about a paper that is due. This paper is very important, people, because whether or not you pass this course will depend a lot on this paper.''

I took notes. She meant what she said. She might be small and mean and have a lisp, but one fact at our school was solid: You wrote a Health paper, and you handed it in on time or you failed Health.

Mrs. Mastriani had to leave class a few minutes early. She said something about meeting the cheerleaders. I felt sorry for the cheerleaders, who have her for a sponsor. She must be loads of fun on the bus on the way to games.

''That woman hates me,'' said Kate as soon as the teacher had left the room.

''Ignore her,'' I said. ''She's a witch.''

''You think so?'' The worried expression in Kate's eyes eased.

''She parks her broom in the supply closet next to the gym.''

Kate giggled. It was a warm, gurgling sound.

''One thing I'd better warn you about,'' I said. ''She's serious about that paper. You have to write it to pass.''

''Don't worry. I copied all the instructions. I can't get a diploma in California without Health.''

''Here either.''

''Look at what else I wrote.'' Kate held out her notebook. The page she showed me was titled very neatly, *HEALTH*. In the upper right corner were Kate's name and the class period, the way notes were supposed to be.

What was written below was nothing on anatomy though. It was a description of Mrs. Mastriani, and not a very flattering description either. After that was the beginning of a story in which Mrs. Mastriani sold pot to elementary school kids.

I was still reading when the bell rang.

Kate snatched the notebook from me. "It's not finished yet," she said. "I'm going to add to it every day, like a diary. I'm going to have her arrested and thrown in jail and have her braces rust off."

"You'd better not let her catch you with that," I said.

"I'm not dumb."

I only saw Kate once more that morning. She was walking in the hall between periods with Amy and Tomo. Kate was on one side of Tomo, and Amy was on the other. Amy looked like somebody's kid sister being dragged along on a date. Neither Kate nor Tomo seemed very much aware that she was there at all.

I must admit that I wasn't the least bit disappointed that Kate and I didn't have lunch the same period. As usual, I ate with Amy, Tomo, and Miranda.

"Where's your cousin?" asked Tomo when I approached the table. His black eyes had a sort of hungry expression. I feared it wasn't for the cafeteria's mystery meat cake, which lay before him on a roll on his tray, soaking up ketchup and looking greasy.

"She has lunch next period." I put down my tray and sat opposite him and Amy. "I told Jason to watch for her."

"Lucky Jason," said Tomo.

Amy shot him a dirty look. Then she leaned across the table at me. "Is that girl for real?" she asked. "Where'd she get those eyes and that hair?"

"Sent away for them at JC Penney's," I said. Then I added, "I don't know. Mom says Kate looks exactly like her mother."

"Who must have been no mutt." Amy chewed at a carrot stick, her teeth small and neat like the rest of her.

"What classes do you have together?" I asked.

"PreCalc and Government," said Amy.

That was when Miranda joined us and we started talking about Homecoming. Miranda was still excited over the dance and The Bank. Evidently she hadn't had the opportunity to meet my cousin yet. Neither had Jason, not till next period lunch. I wondered what he would think of her.

Since we had no classes together, I had to wait to find out until we met at my locker after school. I was there waiting when Jason arrived. "What do you think of Kate?" I asked.

"She doesn't look at all like you described her," Jason told me.

"It's her inner self that shows in photographs."

"She says she knows all about me, that you told her everything."

"Like your name and the fact we attend the same school," I muttered.

"She said I was a lot taller than she expected, and better looking."

"Now, wait a minute!"

Jason laughed. "She was only teasing." He grinned at me, then added, "I told her about our Group 4 project, and she was really interested. She said she'd like to try something like that."

I didn't answer, but I had a weird feeling I knew what Jason was going to say next. The feeling was right.

"I told her that Carl had transferred to Regina and we were one person short in my group. Kate's coming with me to the next meeting."

"That's nice," I said, trying not to sound sour. Jason doesn't like to do much of anything in a gang except Group 4, a school experiment in which small groups of four students do independent study on special projects.

"I told her I would drive her to meetings," said Jason.

What could I say? I didn't want to appear jealous of my own cousin. "That's nice of you," I managed, reflecting how often I practically had to force Jason to go places with me. Now here he was volunteering to entertain a perfect stranger.

I hoped the smile I gave him didn't look as fake as it felt. I was beginning to wonder if maybe Alfred wasn't the only snake that had moved into our house.

4

When some of my friends get depressed, they stay that way for days, weeks even. I figure I'm lucky. My bad moods pass practically as rapidly as they come, and I have to work to keep a depression or a sulk going long enough for anyone else to notice. By Tuesday I was once more convinced that Kate and I could be friends, and by the time Jennifer's party rolled around Saturday night, my misgivings over Kate seemed far in the past.

Jennifer's mother had rented the log cabin in the park from nine until midnight, which was the latest the park board permitted people to use it. Jennifer and Amy and some other kids had gone out there early in the evening, pushed the picnic tables together at one end of the cabin, covered them with white paper, and started a fire in the huge stone fireplace that dominated one entire wall of the room.

When Kate, Jason, and I arrived, Jennifer's parents had already brought in food and were spreading it on the tables. Music was playing on the cassette deck Tomo brought, and flames were leaping and dancing in the fireplace.

Through the scent of woodsmoke, I could catch a hint of damp smell, mixed with the aroma of hot chocolate and the singeing of the marshmallows Sam was toasting.

"Hi, group," said Tomo. He stood next to the fireplace, one arm drooped casually over Amy's shoulders.

The two of them made a stunning couple, I reflected. Tomo was terrific in his natural wool fisherman's knit sweater, his smile wide and handsome, his black hair shiny but warm looking. Next to him, Amy's orangy hair glowed bright, and the black of her sweater picked up the black of his hair. In contrast, Jennifer looked pale and narrow, her light brown hair a fluff around her face.

"Kate, you know Amy and Tomo, Jennifer and Sam," I said.

"Hi," said Kate. Her gaze rested briefly on the girls and Sam, longer on Tomo. His smile became just a bit wider.

I glanced around the room. More kids were arriving, pushing in the door, coming to warm their hands at the fire and to meet Kate.

"How many people did you invite?" I asked Jennifer.

"Twenty. The gang and Steve, Frank, Jamie Peterson." She named more people, all seniors, kids I knew and whom Kate might like. I wandered away from the group to check the food table and to talk with Miranda, then came back with some marshmallows for Jason to toast.

Sam handed his marshmallow stick to Jason and stretched, his hands high above his head.

"Aren't you cold?" I asked. Even though swim

season hadn't begun, Sam was wearing his red T-shirt from swimming. It said FLIERS on the front in white, and SWIMMERS DO IT IN THE WATER on the back in bright blue. The shirt is incredibly ugly, but Sam must like it a lot because he wears it at least once a week.

"Naw," said Sam. "It's hot here by the fire. Besides, I thought I'd better get in the mood, you know? Practice starts the week after next."

"You're a swimmer?" asked Kate, smiling at him.

Sam never needs encouragement to talk swimming. He started in about sprints and splits and stuff like that. He can get pretty boring, but Sam is a super swimmer. He holds our school record in the backstroke.

Jason finished a marshmallow. He gave it to me, then began toasting one for Kate. Over by the double windows, Miranda and Harry were dancing. Jamie Peterson was leaving. Maybe she forgot to turn the lights out on her car.

Sam was now giving his favorite lecture on paring off hundredth seconds. While Jennifer stifled a groan, he rambled on and on about how cutting time is a lot more difficult for backstrokers than for other swimmers, since backstrokers have to do open turns instead of flips.

Jamie came back inside and began dancing with Steve. I glanced at Jennifer. She was sipping hot chocolate. Her eyes held the glazed expression they always assume when Sam talks sports.

"That's fascinating," Kate told Sam.

"The men on Akron Firestone reduce body drag by shaving," said Sam. "Chest, legs, everything. They haven't had a losing season in six years."

Jennifer's eyes gradually grew alert. I suspected she'd heard all of this before.

"Of course I don't think I'd go that far," Sam threw out casually. "The worst drag comes from hair on the head."

"No," muttered Jennifer.

"Carl shaves his head. Every season he shaves his head."

Carl is a distance swimmer. He is the only other recordholder on our team besides Sam.

"Carl doesn't have a girlfriend," pointed out Jennifer, "probably because half the year he's bald."

"Listen," said Sam, sticking out his jaw. "This is important. I could get a scholarship out of swimming."

"Where to? Sea World?"

Don't fight, I thought. Just don't fight, not at the party. With Jennifer and Sam, fighting often seemed a way of life. Sometimes I thought they *liked* fighting.

"Hair grows back," said Sam, running one hand over his dark curls.

"I love curly hair on men," said Kate.

"You do?" said Sam.

"On the other hand, we wouldn't want to endanger a scholarship," said Jennifer.

"I think you'd look fantastic in curls," observed Kate, her greenish blue eyes shifting to Tomo.

"Me?"

We all stared at him.

"Oh, definitely," said Kate. "I know a guy back home who looks a lot like you. He had his hair done, and he looks great."

"What do you know about that?" said Tomo. His arm dropped from Amy's shoulders.

"How would you look in a pink plastic bonnet and curlers?" asked Amy.

"That's only for a couple of hours," said Tomo.

Amy made a noise like a balloon deflating. It

sounded rather rude, especially from someone so dainty.

"Come on, Kate. Here's somebody I want you to meet," I interrupted, dragging her away from the group at the fireplace and across the room toward Miranda and Harry.

Kate already knew Miranda from school, but she hadn't met Harry. As it turned out, they had a lot in common, since both are interested in old cars. Harry is restoring a '72 Camaro, and Kate wanted to hear all about it.

I listened for about fifteen minutes, then went to the food table where I munched chips and dip and a couple of pickles. When I turned to look for Jason, at first I had trouble locating him. He'd left the fireplace and joined Harry, Miranda, and Kate. Amy and Tomo were dancing nearby in a crowd of other kids.

It's a nice party, I told myself, wondering why I suddenly felt depressed. I shook off the feeling and went to ask Jason to dance. When Jason started talking again, I danced with Miranda, Jennifer, and Amy instead. We took turns copying each other's steps, building on the movements, trying to see who could be the wildest. We danced faster and faster, until I noticed Amy had her tongue out in concentration. I started giggling at her, and the others did too.

"What time is it?" asked Amy as we stopped to catch our breath.

"After eleven," said Jennifer, squinting at her watch. "You want a sandwich? Mom made barbecue."

"No thanks. I ate too many marshmallows."

Jennifer opened her mouth to say something, then hesitated, staring across the room. I turned to look.

From where we stood, I had a clear view of the kids near the fireplace: Kate, Steve, Jason, Tomo, and Sam. Tomo was toasting a marshmallow. At least I think that's what he was intending to do. He was holding a stick in the fire, but he wasn't watching, and the marshmallow was blazing.

Tomo was watching Kate. So were Steve, Jason, and Sam. Kate was demonstrating some new dance. Her arms were raised over her head, and she was swinging her body to the music, every now and then stamping one foot to the rhythm.

She brought her arms down and laughed. In a sudden silence from the tape, we could hear the sound clear across the room. Then the next tune started, and we couldn't hear anymore, but we could see Kate's lips move as she said something. Jason raised his hands over his head as Kate had and swung his body.

I closed my eyes. When I opened them again, Jason, Steve, and Sam were dancing with Kate. Tomo had leaned one arm on the mantel and was watching.

"I'll kill him," said Jennifer through clenched teeth.

"They're only having fun," I said. "Besides, you can trust Sam." I glanced at Amy, who was staring at Tomo, then at Miranda.

Miranda was looking at Harry, a big smile on her face. Harry wasn't dancing with Kate. He was stuffing himself on ham barbecue and potato chips.

Bearing a loaded plate, Harry came toward us. "This stuff is good," he told Jennifer. Then he asked, "Is something wrong?"

"Nothing at all," said Amy.

"You guys looks sort of funny. Hey, what's the plan for the football game next week? We going to meet there or what? You girls going to arrange a date for Kate?"

"She might not want a blind date," I said.

"She might even be able to scare up a boy on her

own.'' Amy sounded sarcastic, and sarcasm isn't her style.

A boy? More like four or five boys. As we girls watched with horror, Harry left us to cross the room. He offered his plateful of food to Kate.

Kate selected a single potato chip. She held it for a few seconds between her lips, smiling at Harry before she bit down.

''It's because Kate's new here,'' I said weakly. ''Give her a couple of days, and she'll settle down, find a boyfriend. It won't always be like this.''

Even as I said it, I had my doubts.

5

Nobody asked Kate for a date to the Friday night football game. At the time, I thought maybe the guys were a little afraid of her. Kate was so beautiful and so self-assured. She said what she thought, and what she thought wasn't what the boys expected. I also figured they might be afraid she'd turn them down.

"She wrecks their security," I told Amy. "Boys like to know exactly what a girl is thinking, how she's going to react."

"I don't know about the boys' security," said Amy, "but I know for certain she wrecks mine."

"Come on, Amy. You can trust Tomo. He's dependable."

"As dependable as quicksand."

"Hey. He can't be interested in Kate. She must be four inches taller than he is."

"She slumps a lot," muttered Amy. "Besides, they're the same height sitting down."

"How do you know?"

"Tomo said so." She looked crossly at me. "He also told me Kate likes short men."

"She likes all men," I said. Kate hung on to Jason's every word as if it were the combination code to the United States treasury.

Nothing can shake my faith in Jason, I told myself. Just because Jason was taking Kate to Group 4 didn't mean he was interested in her. Jason hardly ever even looked at another girl, not since the fourth grade when I had punched him in the mouth for kissing Harriet Spengler behind the crawl tunnel.

"What are you grinning at?" asked Jason when he arrived at our house Friday evening.

"I was remembering Harriet Spengler. And what are you grinning at?"

"I got into Oberlin!"

"Oh, Jason!"

He picked me up, hugged me, and swung me around the living room.

"And Kenyon!"

"Both on the same day?"

"Two letters when I got home. Kenyon said they reserve the right to rescind admission if my grades drop or if I take easy courses my last semester of high school."

"So much for Recreational Living," I teased.

"Now if we could talk your parents into letting you go to the same school."

I sighed. My parents are very nice people, but sometimes they can be difficult. They had it in their heads that I should go to a different college from Jason, and nothing I said could change their minds. I could have understood it if my parents didn't like Jason, but they did, so the whole thing seemed silly.

"I'll go to Kent," I said. "We'll have the weekends."

Jason looked down into my eyes. He was about to

say something, or to kiss me, when Kate came into the room.

She curled up on one end of the couch, then asked, "What are you guys celebrating?"

Jason laughed. "I just was accepted at two of the best colleges around, for my specialty anyway."

"What's that?"

"Philosophy, probably," said Jason, letting go of me and spreading his arms wide. "What this world needs is more philosophers."

And people in computers to support them, I thought. If I got a good job in computers, Jason and I could make a great life together, no matter what he studied.

"How about Cal Berkeley?" asked Kate. "One of my dad's friends teaches philosophy there. He won a Nobel prize or something in it."

"I thought of applying there," said Jason.

Jason never told me that! My mouth dropped open. I stared at his back, which was now turned toward me, then past him at my cousin. She had tucked her long legs up under her. The light from the lamp on the end table reflected off her hair, making a bright frame around her face.

"Let's go," I said. "I told Amy we'd be at the game early to get good seats."

"I have an idea," said Kate. "I saw in the paper there's a play on downtown. It's called *Whose Life Is It Anyway?* Why don't we go to it?"

"Tonight?"

"Why not? Who wants to go to a boring old football game?"

"I do," I said.

"Jason?" asked Kate.

"Well—" He turned to look at me, then glanced back at Kate.

"It's the last game of the season, the last football

game of our entire senior year." I couldn't believe it. "Everyone will be there," I said. "Everyone!"

"We wouldn't want to break tradition," said Kate. "We wouldn't want to think we actually had a choice—"

And Kate doesn't have a date, I almost said. I bit it back. "I really want to go to that game," I said in careful tones.

There was a long silence. At least it seemed long to me.

"It was only an idea," said Kate. "Probably the play isn't any good."

"We can go tomorrow night," offered Jason. "I'll call for tickets."

"I promised Amy I'd go to the movies," I said. "We're meeting the gang afterward at Pizza Hut."

"I can take Kate to the play," said Jason. "I wanted to see it anyway."

I was too old to punch him in the mouth, also too shocked. I didn't do anything. I didn't even say anything. I just got my coat out of the closet, and the three of us walked the six blocks to the game.

It was a beautiful evening, not cold, but with a hint of frost in the air. The lights gleamed on the green of the field, and the air rang with shouts and laughter, but I didn't appreciate any of it. I felt a lot like the dessert I'd had at The Bank, warm outside and frozen inside.

The huddles that night weren't only on the football field. Some of them were in the stands, formed around Kate. She was always in the middle of a ring of boys.

Tomo and Sam bracketed Kate like a couple of bookends, and Harry, in front, kept twisting around to smile at her. Since Jason and I sat behind the others in the next row, I had a perfect view of the situation. I also had a good view of the countless times Jason bent forward to talk to Kate.

At halftime the guys gave us girls money, at least some of them did, and sent us for food. They stayed in the stands with Kate, explaining the great American game of football to her as if she'd been an exchange student from Outer Mongolia instead of somebody's cousin from California.

As we waited our turn at the concession stand, we girls were silent. I listened to the excited voices around me and smelled the aroma of hot dogs and popcorn and thought about Kate and the boys. Perhaps I should have agreed to go to the play. Then at least the other girls' dates would have been safe.

When our turn to buy food finally arrived, Jennifer bought a single milk shake. She offered to help the rest of us carry the food, pop, and hot chocolate.

"How come you didn't get more?" asked Amy. Jennifer is a real binge eater. Usually Friday nights she skips dinner and stuffs at the game.

"I only had two dollars, and Sam is broke. He spent all his money on the dance."

"Who gets the shake?" I asked.

"Sam. I'm going to pour it over his head. That will give him something to think about besides Miss California."

"You said your cousin was shy and lonely, and we were supposed to be nice to her," accused Miranda. She was trying to balance two cups of hot chocolate in the crowd, so she couldn't look at me. I was glad of that.

"It's not my fault the boys like her," I said, but no one seemed to believe me.

We made our way silently back to the stands. Near the top of the student section, we could see a cluster of people. We all knew who was in the center of that cluster.

"Why don't you talk to her?" said Jennifer.

"Talk to her? Me? About what?"

"Maybe life is different in California. Maybe she doesn't understand. Tell her how we do things here, that we don't move in on other people's dates."

"You talk to her. I have to live with her." And my parents think she's great, I added silently. It was amazing how fast the two of them sold out for a few clean dishes and a neat bedroom.

"She's your responsibility," said Jennifer. "You invited her in with the gang."

Suddenly I was furious. "What was I supposed to do?" I yelled. "Send her off to play with Jason?"

I didn't know I had yelled so loud until the little huddle of boys parted to see who was doing all the shouting. The only one who kept staring at Kate was Sam, his head cocked to one side like an adoring puppy. We had a good view of his curly black hair and a small part of his face, and that was all.

As we watched, Kate turned to look at Sam, said something, then laughed and rested her head briefly on his shoulder.

"I knew I couldn't trust you," muttered Jennifer.

That was *me* Jennifer was talking about!

"Listen. Just because you can't hold on to your own boyfriend—" I began hotly.

"You always act as if you are so sweet, everybody's best friend—"

"At least I have friends. If it weren't for Sam—" I stopped myself. I couldn't believe it. Here I was, Joni Allen, the girl who always got along with everybody, yelling at one of my oldest friends.

Jennifer didn't answer me. Instead she climbed the stands, taking the steps in long strides. She went right up to the huddle around Kate, raised the shake high in the air, and dumped it over Sam.

The shake was vanilla, thick with ice cream. A big blob of ice cream ran down over Sam's forehead and onto his nose. It hesitated for a second, then plopped into his lap.

Sam blinked. His dark eyes stared up at Jennifer like two lumps of coal in the middle of a melting snowman.

"Oh, no," breathed Amy. Her little face squinched up under the mop of carroty hair. She looked tiny and wizened in her brown coat, no longer pretty, more like a pale-faced monkey.

"Jennifer dumped the shake on the wrong person," said Miranda in disgust.

That last football game was not a success. Our team won all right, 42–13, but I didn't feel very cheery about it. Neither did anyone else in our gang. We sat silently in a sullen little group the whole last half. It didn't help that neither Jennifer nor Sam went home. Sam went to the men's room and tried to wash the shake out of his hair and off his clothes. Then he mostly sat around dividing his stares between the field and Jennifer. Every once in a while, he would spread his hands and say, "What did I do?"

Jennifer didn't answer. She also didn't speak to me.

Neither did Miranda.

Harry kept asking Jennifer and Miranda why they weren't speaking to me, and Jason sat there looking bored except when he was talking to Kate.

"Want to go to Pizza Hut? asked Tomo after the game.

"I'm broke," said Sam. "And sticky."

Jennifer rolled her eyes at the sky.

"I have to go home," said Miranda. "My dad told me to be in early."

"Aw, come on," said Harry. "You never had to go home early before."

"Maybe that's because I always had a good time before."

Evidently Harry thought Miranda was taking a crack at him. "What do you mean by that?" he asked, his eyes narrowed.

"Forget it."

None of us went to Pizza Hut. The other kids stomped off in angry groups of twos. Kate and Jason and I walked home. The two of them talked about Berkeley while I brooded over how fragile my terrific senior year was and wondered how long the other girls would be mad at me.

6

The girls were still angry at me on Monday, and Tuesday, and the rest of the week too. I ate lunch with Amy and Tomo and became used to Jennifer and Miranda not answering when I said hi.

As far as I could tell, Kate didn't notice anything was wrong. She was wrapped up in herself and Group 4 and the letters that had begun to arrive almost every day from Africa, written on tissue-thin paper in envelopes covered with bright stamps. Insulated in her own little world, Kate didn't seem to care about me or my girlfriends.

Thursday evening after school, I worked in my room on endless computer assignments. Finally, so bored I couldn't go on, I took some college brochures from my bottom drawer and spread them before me in a bright array on the blue carpet.

If it weren't for Jason, for wanting to be near him, and for wanting a guaranteed job when I graduated from college, I wouldn't study computers at all. I looked through the brochures and tried to decide what I would select instead. Something to do with math or people—maybe an engineer or a doctor, I thought. I picked up the folder from Case Western Reserve and another from Ohio U. If I went to a good school in premed, would I be able to get into medical school after college? Did I have the background and determination for engineering?

I would never know. Suddenly I jammed all the brochures together and stuffed them back into the drawer. I wound the key on my music box and watched the tiny dancers turn while I chewed at a fingernail. Then I decided to go talk with my mother. She was always ready with a lifeline when I felt lost.

As I bounced down the last two steps and into our living room, I heard voices in the kitchen. My mother was talking with Kate about the Sunday before Thanksgiving. Kate was invited to her mother's relatives. It was only for the day, but she didn't want to go. I hesitated at the bottom of the steps, not wanting to eavesdrop, but not wanting to interrupt either.

"Do I have to?" Kate asked after a couple of minutes of what I call argument but Mom calls discussion.

"These are your relatives, Kathleen. Your mother's family."

"But I don't know them! I haven't even seen them in years. I can't bear the thought of a bunch of strangers pawing over me."

When Mom spoke again, she sounded tired. "I know how you feel, but it's only for one day, a few hours. Listen, your father wrote that he sent you money to buy winter clothes. Suppose we go shopping, get you a new outfit to wear. Would that make you feel better?"

Kate didn't answer.

"These are your mother's parents and her brothers,'' added Mom so quietly I could barely hear the words. ''You are all that they have left of her.''

''All right. I'll go,'' said Kate, but she didn't sound very happy about it.

I didn't know what else they said, because I went back upstairs, abandoning my plan to talk with Mother. What was the sense of it? Next year and college were so far away. I had enough to deal with right now.

Saturday, when Mother asked me to join her and Kate, I said I wanted to stay home to wash clothes and to go see Amy in the afternoon. I never did get around to washing the clothes, but I went over to Amy's house right after lunch. Sitting in her clean, neat bedroom with the white walls and curtains and the dark green carpet, I felt free, as if I could go limp for a while. I lay back in her yellow beanbag chair and closed my eyes, letting all the muscles in my body relax. I hadn't realized I was so tense until I felt them ease one by one: my legs, arms, stomach, the back of my neck, my cheeks.

''You look beat,'' Amy said.

''I'm going to be an old woman by March,'' I mourned. ''Every morning I look in the mirror, searching for the first gray hairs, the wrinkles.''

''Kate's going to be here that long?'' Amy sounded appalled.

''I told you that before she came.''

''I guess I blanked it out of my mind.''

I opened my eyes and stared at the ceiling. Amy had tacked a poster of Rob Lowe up there so that she could lie in bed and stare at him. He looked a little young in the picture, but even more attractive than Jason.

''Somehow it seems completely right that her father is a herpetologist,'' I observed, watching Rob and thinking of Kate.

"He studies herpes?"

I jerked my head up, smiling despite myself. "No. A herpetologist studies snakes. The government gave him money to go to Africa and study snakes."

"Why Africa?"

"I don't know." My muscles were tight again, bunching up. "Maybe they want him to teach the snakes to bite Communists."

"Let's take up a collection and give it to Kate so she can join him," said Amy. "We can put her on a plane and then have a big party to celebrate."

"I think there's something wrong with her," she added when I didn't answer. "Kate can only relate to men. She probably had a warped childhood."

"She can relate to my mother, all right," I said. "Kate relates to Mom so much that we hardly have a chance to talk anymore."

There was a short silence in the room. I'd looked up at Rob Lowe until I developed a crick in my neck. I glanced at the picture of an orangutan Amy has over her desk and then out the window. It was drizzling. The leaves from the trees drifted earthward with the rain, making orange and yellow patterns on the ground.

"Are you jealous?" asked Amy.

She was sitting cross-legged on the floor, her red hair pulled back and caught in a green scarf at the nape of her neck. She had on jeans and one of her brother's old flannel shirts.

"You bet I'm jealous," I said bitterly.

Amy's eyes fell to the carpet, and she picked at a place on one sneaker where the sole was pulling away from the canvas. I didn't have to tell her about last Saturday night. After all, I was with her that Saturday night, her and Tomo. Jason was at the play with Kate.

The movie was a foreign film, from France, supposedly very funny. I had stared at the flickering screen, thinking of my boyfriend out on a date with my cousin. Were they holding hands in the dark like Tomo and Amy? Would he kiss her good-night?

I shook my head violently, trying to clear it of images of Kate and Jason together. Then I cried a little into the tissue I had clutched in my hand. Everyone around me was laughing. The theater was dark and warm and crowded. I had never felt so alone in my life.

"What did Kate say when she got home?" asked Amy, still picking at the sole of her sneaker and avoiding my eyes.

"Nothing. She came sailing in and said hello to everyone, then went upstairs in a cloud of Tempestuous."

"Did Jason say anything?"

It was the first chance Amy and I had had to be alone in weeks. More and more, it seemed as if I had to have an appointment to talk with my best friend. Our phone at home was no longer private, and Amy had made it very clear she didn't want to talk about Kate in front of Tomo.

"Not Saturday night. I didn't even see him. He came over Sunday afternoon." I took a deep breath. "He and I played one long game of chess, and then he and Kate played three. They talked a lot about Berkeley. I sat and listened."

"Sounds like fun."

"I felt like the middle-aged chaperone to some sexy señorita."

"Oh, Joni, what are you going to do?" asked Amy, her small face tight and her eyes filled with worry.

"Slip cyanide in her orange juice."

"I mean for real."

"I don't know."

"Maybe her dad will catch a tropical disease and have to come home."

"The way my luck's been lately, some African government will pay him millions to hang around for the next five years."

That idea was too horrible to consider very long. "I found out why Kate is taking Health," I added. "She failed it in Oakland."

"She dumb or something? Nobody fails Health here unless they don't turn in their paper."

"Kate told Jason it was boring. She said she was too busy to study anything so boring and that all her subjects were much harder than the ones we have here."

"Poor baby." Amy frowned. "Maybe she is stupid. Maybe she doesn't realize she's moving in on our boyfriends. Jennifer was right. You should talk with her, reason with her."

I couldn't believe what I was hearing. Now I was getting a headache. I tried to breathe deeply, evenly, to the count of ten.

"It's your responsibility," pointed out Amy. "The rest of us barely know her. Besides, you have the opportunity. You're with her all the time."

Amy had a point. If anyone was going to talk with Kate, it would have to be me.

"I'll try," I promised. "I'll tell her that we all admire her and want to be friends, but we can't because she's stealing our guys. How's that?"

"Forget the admiration and the friendship part," said Amy. "Just tell her to stay away from our boyfriends."

"Right," I agreed. "Sure. Will do."

7

Like most of the things I'd planned since Kate's arrival, my little talk with her didn't work out the way I thought it would. I had decided to wait until the perfect time when we could be alone, but seeing Kate by myself was every bit as difficult as being alone with my mother.

It wasn't until the Monday before Thanksgiving that the big moment arrived.

Kate was in her bedroom right after dinner, but for a change she left her door open. She was leaving Tuesday after school to spend the holiday with friends in Chicago, and she was poking around in her closet, trying to decide what clothes to take. I hung around in the doorway, waiting like a little kid to be noticed.

"Come on in," said Kate. She had lined up a row of nail polish bottles in front of Alfred's home. She picked one up and shook it. "Do you like this color?" she asked, holding it out.

"Green nail polish?" I thought of saying something witty, like "Halloween was last month," but I restrained myself.

"My cousin Angie gave it to me," said Kate. "She said it matched my eyes."

Cousin Angie. Kate had met this cousin from the other side of her family only the day before, and already they were friends. I had known Kate for weeks and still felt like a member of a hostile tribe.

Without waiting to be asked, I sat on her bed, pulling my legs up and folding them under me. "What was it like yesterday?" I asked.

"Okay." Kate stopped shaking the polish and put it down. She sighed. "It was awful. I felt like some kind of freak. Everybody kept staring at me and talking about my mother as if they expected me to remember her."

"Do you?"

Kate shook her head. "No. Sometimes I think I do. I think I remember a tall woman with hair like mine, picking me up and holding me, at a parade or something; but then it fades, and I'm not sure if I remember or my mind is making it up."

"Like a photograph in an album?"

"No. That's what makes me think it might be a memory. I don't see it; I feel it. The only thing I can see is my mother's hair. The rest is all blurred."

She turned away and moved the nail polish bottles, rearranging them. Alfred shifted slightly and raised his head to look out through the glass. It occurred to me that the room didn't reek as strongly of perfume. Maybe Mom had said something about Tempestuous to Kate.

Now was the time to mention the girls and their boyfriends. I decided to count silently to three and do it. One, two, three.

"Do you know anyone else who has a pet snake?" I asked.

"No," said Kate. "I'm the only one."

"What made you pick Alfred?"

"I didn't. My dad gave him to me as a going-away present at the airport."

Personally I would have preferred a bracelet or a necklace, or even a broken umbrella, but I didn't say so.

"He's a hog-nosed snake," said Kate, rising and leaning over to take the lid off the aquarium. "He's called that because of the funny little snout on the end of his nose." She reached inside and waved her hand in front of the snake. "Look."

Alfred reared up and started to vibrate violently. Then he began to grow larger. He puffed himself up huge and hissed.

I stood transfixed. In a couple more seconds, my troubles would be over. My girlfriends wouldn't have to worry about their guys anymore. Doug wouldn't have to bunk in the family room at Christmas.

"Don't," I managed.

Alfred struck.

He bounced off Kate's hand and fell back into the aquarium.

Kate held her hand out to me. "See," she said. "He's a big fake. He doesn't even open his mouth when he strikes."

I looked at Alfred. He was lying on his back on the floor of the aquarium, perfectly motionless.

"He's dead," I whispered. "He had a heart attack."

"He's a fake," Kate repeated. She reached into the tank, grabbed Alfred by the tail, and flipped him over onto his stomach. Immediately Alfred rolled onto his back again, belly up.

"He plays dead," I said, half to myself. Alfred was pretty cunning. I leaned over the top of the tank. He hardly smelled at all.

Kate replaced the screen and put the rock on top.

She sat on the desk chair. I felt funny hovering over her, so I went back to the bed.

I looked around. Except for the line of nail polish bottles and Alfred, the room looked the same as it had before Kate moved in. She hadn't added any posters to the walls or any stuffed animals to the bed. There weren't any piles of records on the floor or clothes draped over chairs and door knobs to make it seem like home.

"Why don't you put up some posters?" I asked.

"Why would I?"

"Lots of kids do. Amy has a big poster of Rob Lowe on the ceiling of her room so she can lie in bed and look at him."

Kate didn't say anything. Maybe she thought hanging posters of movie stars was childish. Maybe she felt as if she didn't belong in this room.

"Did you pick your subject for your Health paper?" I asked.

"The respiratory system."

"Sounds fascinating."

"I thought I'd pick something noncontroversial. That woman hates me."

"She hates everybody. I picked cancer research."

"Anything I read about cancer makes me think I have it," said Kate.

"Me too," I admitted, "but Mrs. Mastriani should appreciate it. She likes the idea of people in pain."

"Miz Mastriani," said Kate, and we both laughed.

"How's your secret paper coming?" I asked.

"Okay. I'm at the part where Miz Mastriani has cosmetic surgery, and it fails."

"She sees that and she'll really hate you."

"Don't worry. I'm going to wait until I'm safe back in California and then mail it to her."

"You wouldn't."

"You're right. I wouldn't."

I wrapped my arms around my knees and rocked a little on the bed. It was soft and springy, bouncy. I was making wrinkles in the spread, but Kate didn't seem to care. She was smiling at me.

"Did the school give you permission to make up the work you'll miss Wednesday?" I asked. We were having a quiz in Health, and I thought Kate had a test in Literature.

"It's up to the teachers." Kate shrugged. "I just wish I didn't have to skip my Group 4 meeting tomorrow night."

Group 4. Jason. I didn't say anything for a second, but I stopped rocking. Then I said, "Why are you always chasing other girls' boyfriends?"

"Huh?" Kate looked shocked.

"You're always talking to Jason, feeding him stuff about California, about Berkeley and how great it is, playing chess together, and going to Group 4 together."

She flushed. "But he's interested in Berkeley," she protested, "and you liked the idea of Group 4. You said so."

"And eating lunch with him, and going to the play with him." My voice rose. "You're with him more than I am!"

"We're just friends."

"You have all the boys around you. Harry and Sam and Tomo. Why don't you get your own boy-friend? Why are you always trying to steal other people's?"

"I'm not," she said, her voice breathy. "I'm not trying to steal them. They just like me."

"How can they help but like you?" I wailed. "You show up here from California, and you're tall and elegant and beautiful, and you hang all over them like . . . like"—my eyes fell on Alfred—"like a boa constrictor. Of course they like you."

"What do you want me to do?" asked Kate, her eyes blazing and her voice high. "Dress like an old lady and paint zits all over my face?"

"It would do for a start."

Kate stared at me. For a second, I thought she was interested.

"Pretend to be gay," I added recklessly. "That would turn them off."

"You're crazy."

"Chew gum with your mouth open. Stop washing your hair."

"You'd love that, wouldn't you?" said Kate slowly. "All of you. You and your sweet little friends. You're so nice to my face."

"Hey," I said. "Be fair. My friends wanted to like you. They were excited when they found out you were coming here. We thought we'd have loads of fun together."

"When I was only an idea, when I wasn't a real person, someone their boyfriends might like."

I stared at her, wishing I'd kept my mouth shut.

"What they really wanted," began Kate, then changed it. "What *you* really wanted was someone you could feel sorry for, someone you could be generous to, make you seem bighearted."

"That's not true," I said weakly, remembering the pictures of Kate with stringy hair and big glasses.

"You wanted me to be like one of Cinderella's stepsisters, ugly and stupid."

"No," I mumbled.

"I'm not ugly and I'm not stupid," said Kate, standing and saying each word individually, precisely, so I could make no mistake. "And if you and your friends think you can change me one bit—tough luck for you.''

We eyed each other like enemies.

"Please leave my room," said Kate.

There wasn't anything else I could do. I left.

8

Five days without Kate. If someone had asked me before those days how I'd feel about them, I would have said they'd be exactly like the ones before she came into my life.

In many ways they were, at least at first. I didn't tell anyone about our fight, but Amy must have spread the word to the other girls that I was going to talk to Kate, because they seemed to forget they were angry with me. Both Miranda and Jennifer started speaking to me again, and by Wednesday, when two kids from our table in the cafeteria moved elsewhere, Jennifer and Sam joined Amy, Tomo, Miranda, and me for lunch.

Jason came over Tuesday night. It was almost strange seeing him without Kate. We played chess and watched television and later went for pizza. Although it was a school night and I knew my parents wouldn't like my going out, neither of them mentioned it.

''What do you want to do Friday?'' asked Jason the next day when we met at my locker.

"I don't know. Maybe go to a movie. I'll find out what Amy and Tomo are doing."

"Why don't we go by ourselves?" said Jason. "We have a lot to talk about."

Talk about? Somehow that sounded ominous.

I spent as much time dressing Friday as I had for the Homecoming Dance, washing and blow-drying my hair, putting on makeup—especially eye shadow to emphasize my eyes—my new red sweater, and my plaid skirt.

"What are we celebrating?" asked Jason.

"Us," I said, taking his hand.

"Where are your parents?"

"At a party," I said. "They said they'd be home early."

After the movie, Jason suggested we go back to my house; but I wanted pizza, so we went to Pizza Hut. It was almost eleven when we arrived home. I walked slowly through the downstairs, turning on lights, turning up the heat.

Jason plopped on the couch. "Come here," he said.

"Do you want some hot chocolate?"

"I want you to come sit with me."

Why was I nervous? This was Jason, my tall blond boyfriend, whom I'd known ever since I was a baby, whom I'd gone with since the seventh grade. I sat by him.

Jason put a hand on my knee.

I almost jumped out of my skin.

He took his hand away and leaned forward, turning so he could look directly into my face.

"I don't want to go to either Kenyon or Oberlin," he said. "I don't want to go to any college in Ohio."

"Why not?" was all I could think to say. I heard

Jason all right, but it was as if my brain couldn't quite take in what he was saying.

"I've never been anywhere, Joni. I want to get away. I feel as if I'm getting smaller instead of bigger."

"But this is high school. College will be different," I pointed out. "New people, philosophy—"

"I'm going to apply to Berkeley and to Columbia."

"Why?"

"I told you." He spread his hands, then clasped them.

All of a sudden, I wanted to hit him. "Well, don't expect me to go trailing off halfway around the country after you," I said.

"I knew you wouldn't understand."

"I understand," I said bitterly. "I understand that we made plans and now you want to change everything."

"I don't want to change everything." Jason's voice was lower than usual. "Not between us. I want things to be the way they used to be. Remember, when I would come over after school and we'd talk for hours?"

I did remember. I thought of those times, and my eyes misted with tears.

Seeing the tears, Jason leaned close and kissed me. Like always, his lips were soft and warm against mine.

He kissed me again, then sank back against the couch, pulling me with him.

"Please, Joni, try to understand," he said in a low voice. He nuzzled at my ear and kissed gently along the line of my neck toward my shoulder.

"Don't." I sat up and pushed at him.

"Don't?" His eyes followed me. Then he sat straight too, his shoulders stiff under his shirt. "What do you mean, don't? This is the first we've been alone in weeks!''

"My parents will be home any time."

"That isn't the real reason, is it?"

I avoided his eyes. Suddenly I felt very confused. Everything seemed so strange between us, so awkward.

"Joni, half the time I can't find you for the crowd."

"I'm there. You just have to look."

"I don't want to look! You always travel in a big herd of people."

"But I *like* people," I protested. "There's nothing wrong with that."

"There is when you use gangs of them to hide in."

"You believe that?" Didn't Jason know me at all?

"Yes."

"Our friends are important to me," I said slowly, "and I thought they were to you, too."

Jason sighed. "Of course they are. I like our friends." Almost as an afterthought, he added, "I like you too, more than anybody. I like you, but I can't *be* like you."

"And I can't be like you."

"You aren't the same anymore," said Jason.

"Neither are you."

Then, as if he were talking to a perfect stranger, Jason said, "I'd better get going. I wouldn't want your parents to come home and interrupt our love scene."

"You can stay," I offered. "I can make some hot chocolate. We could talk about it."

He looked at me, wavering. Then his mouth tightened into a line. "I don't think so. Not tonight." He leaned over to touch me lightly under the chin with one finger, then brushed my lips even more lightly with his own. "I'll see you in school Monday."

Not tomorrow, not Sunday, but in school Monday.

9

This time I didn't have to crawl out of bed in the middle of the night to go meet Kate. Her flight arrived right on schedule at four in the afternoon. Mom and Dad and I were at the observation window in time to see it taxi to a stop.

Kate was first down the stairs. She waved toward the plateglass window we stood behind, then strode toward the terminal, her new green winter coat flapping open. She had a red scarf wound around her throat and was carrying a long gray mailing tube in one hand and a square pastry box in the other.

"You look like a Christmas tree with legs," I said on impulse as she stepped off the escalator.

"Ho, ho, ho," she said.

I blinked, then caught myself before I blurted out a question. What had happened to Kate's beautiful hair? It was a greasy mess, hanging in strings like in the pictures Uncle Raymond had sent us of her.

Kate noticed my stare and laughed. "Took your advice" she said. By this time, we were at the baggage counter. Dad had her suitcase and cosmetics case, and I grabbed a stack of three boxes held together with string labeled KATHLEEN CANDUSSO in black permanent marker.

"I was joking," I told Kate as we walked to the parking lot. I eyed her with mixed feelings. Under my influence, my cousin was turning into a genuine slob.

"I'll tell you about it later," she said.

Kate seemed glad to see me, not just Mom and Dad, but me. I thought about that on the way home, wondering if Kate had neglected her hair to please me, wondering if she wanted to be friends. I resolved to try harder. Maybe under the beautiful exterior of that tall elegant Californian was a simple naive girl who only wanted to be loved for her virtues.

That idea was so absurd I started giggling. I didn't realize I was giggling out loud until I noticed my mother peering at me over the back of the front seat, a very puzzled expression on her face.

At home I got to play porter again, but at least this time Kate carried the suitcases. I loaded myself with the mailing tube, the big white pastry carton, and the stack of boxes.

"Whew. It's good to be home," said Kate, throwing her suitcases on the bed. Then she glanced at me, the awareness of her remark between us.

"You sound as if you didn't like Chicago."

"I'm glad I don't have to go there over Christmas," she said, crossing to her desk and picking up the two letters from Africa and the one from Oakland, which had arrived while she was gone. I thought she'd open them right away, but she threw them on the desk and leaned forward to stare at Alfred.

"Hello, old buddy. Your usual charming self, I see."

"I fed him yesterday," I told her. "I left the room

for about thirty seconds, and he polished off the egg before I got back.''

"Told you he's a sneak." Kate shoved her suitcases toward the head of her bed. "Have a seat."

"Thanks." I flopped, legs dangling, and watched her. I knew it was rude, but I couldn't keep my eyes off her hair.

Kate picked up the mailing tube, reached in one end, moved her fingers around, and slowly drew out the contents. It was a large poster. She went back to the desk, leaned over Alfred's aquarium, and held it against the wall.

The poster covered the Degas dancers that hung there, and more. It must have been three feet wide and two feet high.

"What do you think?" asked Kate.

"Great," I said. I wasn't certain what I thought. The poster was a big reproduction of a painting, mostly made up of big blobs of black color, some white, and a large area of yellow.

"Do you think Aunt Lois would mind if I moved the dancers over the nightstand and put this here?"

"She won't mind at all," I said slowly. "She'll be glad you put up something you like." I stood. "I'll get some tacks."

"Shouldn't we ask?"

"Are you kidding?" I grinned. "I've discovered that tack first, ask later, is the best policy."

I held one end of the poster while Kate tacked the other, then moved to the middle to keep it flat while she finished. We stood back to survey the results.

The reproduction appeared stark at first, black and white against the white walls, severe in contrast to the fluffy fall of curtains at the windows. Then I noticed how the yellow blob picked up the yellow in the bedspread and how the black echoed the black frame of the aquarium on the desk beneath the poster.

Kate turned toward the bed, shifting the suitcases and beginning to unpack the larger one first. The contents were as neat as usual. She hung her jeans and skirts and tops in the closet, put underclothing in her dresser, and slid her shoes onto the shoe rack on the closet floor.

"None of your clothes are dirty," I observed.

"Mrs. Harrison washed them yesterday. She hasn't been able to find a job in Chicago, and I think she's bored." Kate pulled two records from the bottom of the suitcase and eyed them. They were alike, two copies of a record called *Dave Digs Disney*.

"This is a reissue," she explained. "My dad loves it. His record is ancient and covered with scratches. I bought one for him for Christmas, and one for me to keep."

"Doug said his room is being turned into a double next quarter," I told her. "His roommate has a stereo, so Doug's bringing his home at Christmas for you to use if you want it."

"I wish I had my records here," she said, putting the two new ones on her desk.

"You can borrow mine."

"Thanks. I love music. I always used to study to it." She wrinkled her nose. "Probably why my grades were so bad."

"You had bad grades?"

"Not all that bad, but I'm not the superbrain you are."

"I'm no brain!" I couldn't believe she said that.

"You sure are, compared with me anyway. You take Calculus and German. You even get A's in them."

So I got the brains in the family, and Kate got the beauty. I'd trade. That reminded me of her hair.

"I really was joking when I said you should stop washing your hair and chew with your mouth open," I said.

"I know, but it was a great idea. That's what I meant when I said you have brains. Your idea was the only reason I survived in Chicago."

"At the Harrisons'?"

"Right." She picked up the pastry box, opened it, and peered inside. "Want a doughnut?"

"Yes." I wiggled on the bed, almost upsetting her empty case. I pulled the lid down and leaned on it, taking the glazed doughnut she offered. "Tell me about it," I demanded. "I thought you liked those people. I thought you'd rather have stayed with them than here."

"Hey." She sat on the desk chair and took a bite from a doughnut, chewing carefully and swallowing before she continued. "I actually prayed I wouldn't have to live with the Harrisons. I worried more about staying with them than about my dad's going off to Africa and leaving me behind."

"What's wrong with them?"

"Nothing with Mr. and Mrs. Harrison. It's their son, Arnold. Icky Arnie, the twenty-four-hour grossout. Ugh." She shuddered. "He's a human octopus."

"What's a human octopus?"

"Someone with eight arms, all attached to hands."

"Oh." I was beginning to get the picture.

"He's eighteen, has an Olympic case of zits, and can't keep a single hand to himself. Talk about lechers—" She shook her head and took another bite of doughnut.

"Why didn't you tell your father?"

"I wanted to." She made a disgusted face. "I

probably would have if the Harrisons hadn't moved to Chicago, taking Arnie with them. But my dad is sort of innocent, you know.''

"No, I don't know." Uncle Raymond had never even sent a single picture of himself. I wouldn't recognize him if I fell over him in the living room.

"Sometimes I think Dad's spent so much time studying snakes that he doesn't know very much about people.''

"Couldn't you tell Mrs. Harrison?''

"Are you kidding? About her precious Arnie? It was safer to take your advice. Believe me, I owe you.''

"What did you do?''

"Well, I thought of telling Arnie I was engaged, but that wouldn't have made a bit of difference to him, so I settled on being repulsive." She laughed. "Over Toledo, I went into the lavatory on the plane and changed into a dirty blouse with a ripped shoulder seam. I put a big wad of gum in my mouth and rubbed some hand cream into my hair.''

"I see," I said. I could, too.

"Mrs. Harrison was appalled. She kept talking about how a person had to keep their chin up during life's hard times and not become too depressed even when they're separated from their loved ones.

"Then she talked a lot about how if a person showered and washed their hair, they would be a lot happier both physically and mentally." Kate paused. "I felt sorry for her. By the end of the visit, she was lecturing about mental health centers and school counselors. One of the reasons I let her wash my clothes was to give her hope for my future.''

"What about Arnie?'' Remembering my doughnut, I shoved the rest of it into my mouth and watched Kate while I chewed.

"Would you believe that at first he didn't notice I had changed?" She made a face. "He was all hands, the same as ever. He'd come around with these slimy smiles and talk about Oakland as if we'd been lovers there or something. Once he tried to grab me, but I gave him the old elbow in the stomach routine."

"Is he dangerous?" I'd never known a human octopus, although some guys came pretty close.

"No, he's only repulsive," said Kate. "I used to feel sorry for him. That was a mistake. I'd say hi to him in the halls between classes. He decided I was in love with him."

I thought of how Kate hung all over boys and wondered if she realized how much she flirted with them.

"By Wednesday night old Arnie was finally beginning to get used to the idea. He started treating me like a kid sister." She stretched, then lowered her right hand until it grazed the top of her head. "Ugh. I feel like a street person. What I need is a long hot shower and about ten shampoos. . . ." She hesitated, then slid her green eyes at me, grinning. "Or do you want me to stay this way until March?"

"Well—"

"Joni!"

"Shower," I said quickly. "Shampoo." Maybe Kate and I could work out a truce. Maybe I could even learn to like her.

10

The boxes Kate brought from Chicago contained Christmas presents. Several days after she came home, they appeared on the floor next to her desk, brightly wrapped in shiny red paper with large intricate bows.

One evening, while Kate was at Group 4 with Jason, Mom and I went on a shopping excursion. I wrapped my packages in paper featuring gingerbread men and Santa Claus, with ribbons of yarn, and stowed them under my bed along with last year's dust fuzzies. Even Mom lacks the courage to look under my bed.

The smallest gift I bought was for the Foreign Language Club grab bag. This year we were buying unisex trinkets for under five dollars. The only catch was that the trinkets had to come from one of the countries whose language was taught in our school: Germany, France, or Spain. In a gift shop, I'd found a set of wooden nested egg-people made in West Germany and wrapped them in paper proclaiming *Stille Nacht, Heilige Nacht*.

Way back in September, I had volunteered to be in

charge of the Foreign Language Club Christmas party. At our last meeting, we had discussed the party and gift exchange. Now, during lunch period and before school in the morning, I tracked down other members and reminded them of their promises to buy a piñata and to bring German, French, and Spanish foods. I borrowed records of French carols from Mrs. Mason, and Spanish and German ones from my German teacher, who also teaches Spanish.

Amy volunteered to have the party at her house. I asked the foreign exchange students from our school, one Swedish and one Japanese, to be special guests. Then all I had to do was talk Jason into skipping a Group 4 meeting to go with me to the party.

Arranging for the party was fun. It took my mind off Jason's and my troubles, and the fact that ever since our fight we'd been pretending that things were like always, when they weren't at all. It also took my mind off my eternal problems with Computers. That is, it did until the second Wednesday in December when I once more went to Mr. Farraccio's room after school for help.

"How's my favorite student?" he teased as he came into the room several minutes later, carrying coffee in a Styrofoam container.

"Lost again," I muttered.

"I'm sure we can fix that in no time," he said with a show of optimism.

He was right. It took all of ten minutes to solve my problem.

"See," said Mr. Farraccio. "That wasn't so hard."

"I don't know why I have so much trouble in class," I said.

"I know why." Mr. Farraccio leaned back in his chair and sipped at his coffee. He had loosened his blue necktie. I stared at the knot hanging below the open collar button to avoid his eyes. "It's called daydreaming."

I blushed, feeling blood climb my forehead and make my ears glow beneath my hair.

"I'm sorry," I said.

"Last year you made straight A's in Computers. It was as if you couldn't wait to get to class."

"That was different. It was like a game. It was fun."

"And this isn't fun anymore."

"No, it isn't." I looked him right in the eyes. "I guess I don't relate very well to machines."

Mr. Farraccio studied the Styrofoam cup. Then he looked back at me and folded his arms across his chest. "Joni," he said, "you know I like you and I like having you in my class. But are you absolutely certain that this is what you want, this future as a computer programmer?"

I didn't answer. I was too depressed.

"Your statement about not relating well to machines has a lot of truth in it," he said. "Have you thought about it?"

"Not really." Now I sounded depressed too. Life was full of problems: first Kate, then Jason, now this. Just when I'd decided everything in my life was settled, things started to fall apart.

"Have you considered alternatives?"

"Well—I think of being a doctor or maybe an engineer, but I don't know."

"And how do you feel about being a full-time computer programmer?"

"To be perfectly honest," I admitted, "I hate computers."

Mr. Farraccio laughed. "You could have fooled me," he joked. "Suppose I give you a drop slip for next semester, and you concentrate on finding a career you might be happy in?''

I might hate computers, but I liked the computer teacher, I thought as I carried the note he'd given me to the guidance office. Mr. Farraccio is a very understanding person.

When we met leaving the building, I told Jason I was dropping Computers, but he didn't seem to think it was very important. He only nodded, his mind apparently a thousand miles away.

"Are you going to the swim meet tomorrow night?" I asked, trying to get back on familiar ground with him. "It's at home."

"There's Group 4."

"Oh." I pretended to be looking for an assignment in my notebook, flipping it open and closing it again. It seemed Group 4 was always meeting lately. Or was it just Jason and Kate?

"I could stop by after," he said, "when I drop Kate off."

"Don't bother," I told him. "Those meets last forever, and I always get a headache from the heat and the noise."

"Tell you what," he said, leaning against the outside wall of the gym and looking down at me. "Why don't I come over this evening? You and I can go for a long walk, the way we used to before I got my driver's license."

His eyes were the exact shade of blue of the sweater I'd bought him for Christmas, I noticed with detachment. I had wrapped it more carefully than my other presents and put it on the shelf in my closet instead of under my bed.

"I can't. Kate and I are going to the library to work on our Health papers."

"Okay." He straightened, his face going into shadow.

I put out a hand and touched him on the arm. "Listen," I said, "I can ask Mom to drive Kate. I'll have plenty of time to work on the paper over vacation."

"I just remembered I promised Tomo I'd go to karate class with him."

"Karate? You?"

"No," said Jason, his usual smile crossing his face. "This is Tomo's first lesson, and he said he could bring a friend. I'm providing moral support."

Since I knew that Kate was going to Group 4 with Jason, I didn't even ask her to come to the swim meet. Why should she go out with me when she could go out with my boyfriend? Instead, I made arrangements with Jennifer to pick me up at seven.

We chose central seats in the balcony over the pool and sat staring at the water, waiting for the other kids to join us and the teams to come out and start warm-ups.

"Do you really hate swimming?" I asked Jennifer. "Or are you only teasing Sam when you complain about it?"

Jennifer looked directly at me. "I hate it," she said. "I never did like water except to drink or to wash in. I think I'm allergic to chlorine and that all that water softens Sam's brain. I also don't like the fact that after the meet's over, Sam will come to my house, and we'll sit on the couch, and he'll fall asleep and start snoring."

"I guess that answers my question."

"Sometimes I have nightmares," said Jennifer. "Sam and I are married. We have three children, and they're all swimmers. I am a Swim Team Mom."

At that moment our team came out of the locker room. They walked around the pool slowly, then began exercises, stretching and bending, loosening muscles. Several minutes later Amy and Tomo joined us in the bleachers and then Miranda and Harry. Harry was wearing a little red airplane pin that said FLIERS.

When the other team appeared, there were yells and catcalls across the pool. Then all the swimmers entered the water and started swimming laps. The noise had already begun. My blouse was too warm. I glanced at Jennifer, who was wiping her forehead with a tissue.

On the other side of me, Amy was sitting with her hands over her ears, her eyes bright with excitement. Next to her, Tomo screamed, although these were only warm-ups.

A whistle cut through the sound, closing my ears and bringing the teams from the water. As the PA system came on, my ears opened, and I sat listening to the names of coaches and schools and then the names of the swimmers for the first race.

Those swimmers advanced to the blocks, shaking their arms and legs. They climbed onto the blocks, leaned over to take their marks, and almost grabbed ankles.

As the starter pistol exploded, the crowd surged to its feet. I stepped onto the seat in front of me, stretching tall to see over other people.

"Go, go!" shouted Amy.

I thought I heard Tomo whistling, but the sound was lost in screams and cheers. Someone lurched into my right side, almost knocking me over. It was Jennifer, jumping and pounding me on the arm.

We took first and fourth places. I flopped back on

the seat, exhausted. "I thought you hated swimming," I said to Jennifer.

She gave a twisted little smile. "I'm in training to be a Swim Team Mom."

11

Just before Christmas vacation, Tomo acquired curls. Actually, he had his hair permed right after school on the twenty-second, so he showed up that night at the Foreign Language Club Christmas party with a new image.

"It makes me taller," he said to Amy. "Don't you think it makes me taller?"

"Maybe a little bit," she conceded. "It looks a lot better than I thought it would."

Curls did look good on Tomo. They brought out the square craggy structure of his face and the merry twinkle in his dark eyes.

"Where'd you get that done?" asked the exchange student from Japan, a small, thin boy with glasses.

"Hair Today, Hair Tomorrow."

The exchange student looked thoughtful.

About that time, Mrs. Mason arrived and put on a record of Spanish carols. Then Jennifer came, explaining that Sam couldn't make it. Miranda brought a big platter of croissants filled with nuts, and a sophomore boy I didn't know brought a German cheesecake.

Soon the long table covered with a red paper cloth was filled with cookies and cakes and dishes of nuts and candy. Tomo and his hair were forgotten as kids crowded around the goodies.

"Glad you skipped Group 4?" I asked Jason.

"Sure," he said, but he didn't sound very happy about it, and I wondered if he was being totally honest. He dug through a bowl of mixed nuts, picking out the almonds, then asked, "Who made the fruitcake?"

"I did. I brought it over after school when we decorated for the party. The fruitcake is an old European custom, more for New Year's than for Christmas. There are little things baked into it, like a thimble and a ring and a penny, to signify what is coming for you in the new year."

"You bite down on one and get a twelve-month toothache."

"Right." I cut a piece and chewed cautiously. There was nothing in my piece except for raisins and nuts and candied fruits.

The party was picking up. Mrs. Mason had put on German carols, and a group of kids was standing by the fireplace, singing, swinging their mugs of hot chocolate like tankards.

I eyed the room with satisfaction. The basket of grab-bag gifts near the door overflowed. Dangling from a hook in the center of the ceiling was the piñata, a snowman, revolving slowly from the movement beneath him.

"Are you coming over Christmas Eve?" I asked Jason. That was when we always exchanged our presents.

Jason frowned. "I was going to tell you—" he began.

"What?"

"I can't. We're leaving for my grandparents' in Minnesota the twenty-fourth."

"Oh," I said, very quietly.

"I'll be home two days after Christmas. We can exchange our gifts then."

I nodded, trying to adjust to Christmas Eve without Jason. He wouldn't be in any of the pictures, I realized. I avoided looking at him, watching Steve instead. Steve came beside me, giving a big smile, and looked at the fruitcake.

"Who made that?" he asked.

"I did," I said, trying not to sound gloomy.

Across the room, the German record had finished, and some kids were arguing over what to play next. There was one of those sudden silences that sometimes comes in a crowd.

"Yeouch!" howled Steve. He poked into his mouth with two fingers, an expression of pain on his face.

I tried to look innocent and harmless.

"There was a thimble in this cake," mumbled Steve.

"It's a symbol," I explained. "The New Year's cake is filled with small objects: a thimble, a ring, more. It tells what the new year will bring you."

"What does a thimble have to do with anything?" he muttered, eyeing the mashed piece of metal on the palm of his hand.

"It means you're going to have to do all your own mending," I told him.

Steve grinned. Then he narrowed his eyes at me, as if he'd never really seen me before. "What did you do with your hair, Joni?" he asked.

"Cut it." Actually Kate had cut it, into long bangs

that swept back over the tops of my ears, then fell straight to my usual length in the back. The cut was sophisticated for me, and what was better, it made my eyes seem huge.

"It looks terrific," said Steve.

Steve had nice eyes himself, I thought, a soft warm brown, not quite as dark as mine. I glanced sideways at Jason. He hadn't seemed to notice Steve and I were talking. He hadn't noticed my hair either.

At ten, we took turns at the grab bag, and then all that was left of the party was the piñata. By that time everyone was making so much noise that the stereo was only a small undercurrent of sound in the chaos. Mrs. Mason turned it off. I climbed on a chair and waited for silence. That didn't work. Finally someone turned off all the lights for about three seconds. When they flashed back on, I said very loudly, "It's time to break the piñata. One of the grab-bag gifts has a little silver star pasted on it. The person with the star breaks the piñata."

I turned over my grab-bag gift, a tree ornament of an angel with silver and gold sparkles on her wings. It had no silver star, nor did Jason's party whistle.

"I got it!" yelled Tomo. "Right here! Make way, everybody! I get to break the piñata!"

Beside me, Jennifer whispered, "My piece of cake had a gold ring in it. What does that mean?"

"A wedding."

A big circle cleared in the middle of the floor. Mrs. Mason and Amy began to spin Tomo. He turned, blindfolded, a broom handle clutched in his hands.

They stopped spinning him, aimed him the direction of the piñata, and said, "Go!"

"Hi-ya!" screamed Tomo. He raised the broom handle over his head like a club and charged.

Tomo ran straight across the room and into a wall, knocking himself flat on the floor.

"That's not how it's done," said Mrs. Mason.

Two kids got Tomo back on his feet and aimed him toward the piñata again. This time he didn't run. Instead he approached slowly in a crouch, the handle extended and swinging viciously.

There were screams and gasping sounds as people scattered before him. He turned and sprang, bashing into Harry and knocking him into the refreshment table.

Amy hid behind the couch. As Tomo thrust violently before him, a whole gang of kids ran for the relative safety of the stairs.

Tomo wheeled, panting heavily, and still in a crouch stalked the opposite direction.

"Stop him before he kills someone!" yelled Mrs. Mason.

Nobody was interested in stopping Tomo. They were only interested in keeping out of his way. I wasn't worried about anyone's getting hurt though. I could see that the blindfold had slipped off the corner of his right eye. Through the gap, Tomo was eyeing the piñata.

He took one step sideways, then another. Now he was directly under the dangling snowman.

"Hi-ya!" Tomo screamed, leaping straight into the air.

The snowman split, spilling a shower of candy and gum, whistles, and other small toys. While the kids scrambled around him, snatching the treats, Tomo stripped off his blindfold and stood proudly in the center of thc shower.

It was more fun to watch than to take part. Jason must have thought so too, because he stayed to watch by my side.

'Are you on the clean-up committee?'' he asked. His voice sounded low and soft, almost sad.

"Not this time." I reached and caught his hand.

"Then let's go."

Outside, the world was white. A soft covering of snow lay over the walks, the trees, the houses. Jason had to clear the windshield before we could leave. I stood on the sidewalk and stared up into the sky. It wasn't cold. I stuck out my tongue and caught a snowflake on it, then another.

The roads were slippery, but Jason is a good driver. He pulled up in front of the house next to ours, which was for sale and had been standing empty for months.

"Want to come in?" I asked.

"Let's sit out here," he said, turning toward me on the seat. For a second I thought he wanted to tell me something. But then, instead, he put an arm around my shoulders and pulled me close.

I put my head on Jason's shoulder, and he rested a cheek on top of my hair. After a while, it grew cold in the car. We could see our breath steaming before us as the snow built up gradually on the windshield. For a little while, the whole world was shut away from Jason and me.

12

The day after Christmas, I received catalogs in the mail from Case Western and Ohio U. I spent the afternoon poring over them and filling out application forms. Mom promised to drive me to Case Western to see the school some Saturday, and I extracted a promise from Dad to take me to Ohio U. over spring vacation.

The next day—the day Jason was to come home from Minnesota—I spent at the library, organizing my notes for my Health paper, writing the bibliography, and beginning the rough draft. Kate didn't come with me. She said she was going to stay home to work on her final draft at her desk.

"Some student," I teased when I saw her before dinner. When I'd arrived home at four, Kate was gone, and her desk was bare. She hadn't come in until after five, her hair windblown and her cheeks rosy from the cold.

"I needed a break," she said. "I went for a walk."

"Are you going to work on your paper this evening?'' I asked. What I really wanted to know was if Kate was going to be home. I didn't want her hanging around while Jason and I exchanged presents.

''Kate's going to the movies with Mom and Dad and me'' came a voice from behind me. I turned and almost bumped into Doug, then smiled at him. It was easy to smile at Doug. He has dark brown hair, like mine only curly, and brown eyes, and one of the most agreeable faces I've ever seen. When I was little, I used to pretend we were twins, which was silly, because Doug is two years older than I am.

''Aren't you, Kate?'' he added, looking past me. ''I think Jason and Joni probably have some kind of plans of their own.''

Kate nodded, then looked down at the table, her eyes straying to the candles and greens in the center of it. She touched a place mat, then ran a fingernail along the crease in a napkin.

Kate didn't seem very happy, maybe because Jason and I were going to be alone together. I glanced at Doug in time to catch a huge wink.

It's great to have a big brother, even if he is away at college most of the time. It's especially great, since my big brother always seems to be on my side. As I headed for the kitchen to collect more silverware and plates, I was wishing that I still felt that way about Jason, that he was always on my side.

When Jason called me that evening, he sounded tired and far away. He said he didn't think he could come over that night, and then he said he would, and then he didn't know.

''Suit yourself.'' I resisted the urge to slam down the receiver. ''Everyone else went to the movies, but I stayed home waiting for you to call. I'll just sit around here working on my Health paper while you decide whether you want to see me or not.''

''I'll be there in about ten minutes,'' he said, a total lack of enthusiasm in his voice.

Maybe Jason wasn't feeling well. I hung up and stood, one hand on the receiver, chewing on my bottom lip. At the moment, I was writing the section of my paper on leukemia, which strikes a lot of people our age. One of the first symptoms was fatigue.

The phone rang under my hand. I picked up the receiver, and it was Steve.

''You said you made that cake for the party, the one with the thimble in it,'' said Steve.

''You want some advice on picking out a pattern.''

''Not exactly.''

''You lost a tooth, and you're going to sue.''

Steve laughed. ''I told my mother about the cake, and she wants to make one for her New Year's party. Is it a special recipe?''

Steve's voice was deep and rumbly. I sat on the stool next to the phone and read off the recipe. Then Steve asked me about my Christmas, and I asked about his. He had gone to the mountains in upstate New York, on a skiing vacation.

''I've never been on skis,'' I admitted.

''Hey, there's nothing like it. There's a slope with artificial snow about an hour north of here. You ought to try it some time.''

''I'd love to.''

''You can rent equipment. Tell you what: Some weekend we can get a bunch of kids together, make a skiing party.''

At that moment, the doorbell rang. I told Steve a party was a great idea, then ran to answer the bell, my mind full of snow and skis and the gang laughing together in their attempts to stay upright.

Jason stood on the mat, brushing snow from the shoulders of his jacket and out of his blond hair. He stepped inside, unzipping his jacket.

"Want me to hang it up?" I offered. He was pale, and there were dark shadows under his eyes.

"I can't stay long. I see you still have lots to do." He nodded at the pile of note cards, the spill of handwritten papers across the coffee table where I'd been working.

I made a face. I thought of sitting next to Jason on the couch, but remembering the last time we'd been there alone, I circled the table and flopped on the big floor pillow I'd been using to do my work.

"You didn't sound very happy on the phone," I said.

He shrugged. "I guess I'm tired. We've been on the road most of the day."

We sounded like strangers again, making conversation. I slid a stack of notes to one side and folded my hands on the table, looking up at him opposite me on the couch.

Jason *was* good-looking, tall and slender and blond. He usually had a smile on his face and laughter in his blue eyes, but that evening he didn't look like he wanted to laugh. I had a sudden stab of fear, remembering the section on leukemia in my Health paper. Were his pallor and fatigue and those dark circles a sign of some terrible disease? Jason hadn't been himself lately, not even the night of the Foreign Language Club party.

"Is everything all right?" I asked.

"Sure."

"I have your present." I got to my feet, took his present from under the tree, and gave it to him, then returned to the distance of my pillow.

"Thank you," said Jason when he saw the sweater. "That's a great color."

"It matches your baby blue eyes," I teased.

Jason gave a sickly smile.

"Jason, I know there's something wrong," I said, fear clutching at me again.

"No," he said. Then "Yes."

He *was* sick. I wanted to get up and run around the table and throw my arms about him. Instead, I pressed my hands tightly together. I had to know the worst first.

"What is it?"

"I think maybe we ought to break up," he said, his words so low I could hardly hear him.

For a moment, my heart seemed to stop. Then I realized that Jason didn't have cancer or any other deadly disease.

"Is that all?" I asked.

"Is that all!" He shot up straight, staring at me, the box with the sweater falling to the floor.

Then I did get up and run around the table and throw myself on the couch beside him. He moved so there was a space between us, as if I had bad breath or didn't shower.

"Oh, Jason. I was so scared. I thought you were sick. I thought you had cancer."

"Cancer?" His mouth dropped open.

"You were so serious, and you're pale, and—"

Jason closed his mouth, opened it again, and closed it again. Then he began smiling. He shook his head and leaned back on the couch. "Cancer," he repeated.

"It's horrible. I can hardly stand to write my paper."

"Worse than breaking up." He slid his eyes at me, grinned, then started laughing. He grabbed me and hugged me, then let go to look at me very seriously. "What am I ever going to do without you, Joni?"

"I don't know," I said. "I guess you'll just have to try to stumble along."

"Yeah," said Jason, still watching me.

I dropped my eyes. That's me, I told myself, Joni Allen, making a joke when my whole life, my whole future, is breaking apart. I blinked rapidly, fighting tears.

"I didn't want it to end like this," I said. "I didn't want it to end ever, really." I remembered the first time we'd actually gone on a date together, in the seventh grade, to a dance at the youth center. "Do you think we've outgrown each other?"

"I think we've grown—differently," said Jason.

I didn't answer. I still was afraid I might cry.

"I have something for you," Jason said, standing and reaching into a jacket pocket.

"No."

"It's your Christmas present." He took out a little box. "I bought it the Saturday after the Homecoming Dance."

"I don't need a present." I looked at my hands, wanting to hide them behind my back, not wanting to take the box. "Can't you return it?"

"I don't want to return it. I bought it for you." Jason held his right hand out, palm up, the little box on it. It wasn't wrapped. The outside was gray velvet.

I ducked my head, suddenly shy.

"Joni—"

I took the box and opened it. Inside, on purple silk, was a ring, really two rings, two smooth gold circles with tiny hands intertwined with each other.

"It's beautiful," I said.

"Please take it."

"Thank you," I said. I closed the box. Please go, I shouted inside myself. Please go before I cry.

As if he heard me, Jason zipped his jacket. He picked up the sweater and the box, put on the lid, fumbling at it. "Well," he said, sounding lost, "I guess I have to go now."

"Do you have to?" I heard myself ask.

"Yes, I have to." Our eyes met briefly, and he added, "See you." Then he was gone.

I sank down on the couch, waiting for tears. My eyes ached, and my vision blurred, but I didn't cry. I opened the box and took out the ring, trying it on. It was a perfect fit. I took it off and stared at it. Between my fingers the tiny hands slipped apart, and the pieces separated. I held two individual rings.

13

Jason and I were a lot like the rings. We had parted, and now I had to become a separate person. The trouble was, I didn't want to be a separate person. I sat in my bedroom, staring at the couple on the music box for hours, listening to its tiny tinkling tune and trying to understand what had happened. The music was playing, the figures going round and round, but I wasn't dancing with Jason anymore.

Sometimes I opened the velvet box to look at the rings and think of Jason and me, feeling sad and empty and confused. Then my throat would ache as I sat there with a hard, heavy feeling in my chest. I cried a lot those days, all by myself in my room. Finally, one snowy afternoon I took the music box and the rings and put them in my middle drawer, back behind a stack of clothes where I couldn't see them anymore.

After Jason and I broke up, nothing important happened the rest of that vacation; but somehow the days crawled by, one after another. Steve called, and we planned a skiing date, but it never came off—at least not over the holidays. Miranda had a New Year's party, and I went to the movies with Amy and Tomo, but nothing seemed to make much of an impression on me. I guess I was trying to sort things out, to adjust to the fact that life wasn't going the way I'd thought it would, with all the important events already settled.

It was a relief when school started and I could go back to classes and the cafeteria, to hearing Jennifer grumble about the swim team and watching Tomo demonstrate his new karate chops over lunch.

Then something very odd occurred. I don't know if it was the shock of breaking up with Jason or the new way I'd been thinking about my life, but it was as if what happened around me became clearer. I don't mean I saw it better, although at times it almost seemed that way. I mean it was more focused. I was more aware of my friends and what they did according to their inclinations, not just in relation to me.

For instance, I noticed more of the true Amy instead of only Amy as my friend. I'd always thought of her as quiet and a little shy, but she wasn't really. She was quiet, but she was in contact with most of the other kids and their situations. I became aware of the fact that Jennifer might grumble about swimming and being a Swim Team Mom, but she was perfectly willing to accept it as her future. And that behind Miranda's vacant-looking blue eyes was a brain that picked up top grades in science and math.

Jason missed most of the first week of school after vacation. Some strain of the flu was working its way through the Midwest, and Jason caught it. He was one of the first kids in our school to come down with it, and definitely the first in our gang.

Jason's being absent made everything easier for

me. I didn't have to run into him in the halls and speak as if we were two mere acquaintances, or listen to Tomo recount stories of Jason and Kate together in classes. Also, I could pretend when I went to my locker that Jason would be there if he weren't lying home in bed, blowing his nose and fighting a fever.

During that week, tall, elegant, cool Kate seemed to grow pale and grouchy. Circles appeared under her green eyes, dark circles that not even her makeup could cover. She'd caught a cold. For two days it amused me to see her snuffling into a tissue, her nose red and her eyes teary like any other normal human being. Then she began to complain of a headache.

By the weekend, Kate was in bed, coughing and blowing her nose between bouts of restless sleep. I was on the chicken soup and cheerful visitor detail. I lugged endless glasses of juice, cups of hot tea, boxes of tissues, and magazines up the stairs.

Although I still hurt from losing Jason, it bothered me to see Kate sick like that. She seemed so fragile, so lacking in spirit that it was hard to think of her as the competition.

She spent practically the entire week in bed. Even the three letters from Africa and the Christmas package that finally arrived from her friends in Oakland couldn't raise her spirits.

Thursday when I went to Kate's room to pick up her dinner tray, she was sitting up in bed. For the first time in days, she'd eaten her dinner. She'd even finished the prunes Mom had put in a side bowl.

"When do you think you can go back to school?" I asked, putting the tray on the desk next to Alfred and flopping into her desk chair. By that time I'd decided if I were going to get the flu, I would have already. A few more germs weren't going to change anything. I ran my fingernails over the screen on Alfred's aquarium.

Alfred lifted his head at the noise and stared out through the glass at me, flicking his little forked tongue.

"Boo!" I said.

Alfred vibrated his tail and puffed himself up. He was probably hoping I'd play dead.

"Monday, I guess," said Kate. She didn't sound especially eager.

"You want me to take in your Health paper tomorrow? Miz Mastriani said if we're on the operating table, one of the nurses had better run it over."

"It's there, in my stack of books." She waved in the direction of the desk, coughed, and sat up straighter. "I hope she's satisfied. I spent days on that thing." Her voice was stronger, clearer, almost normal.

"You sound better," I said. "You look better too." That last part was a lie, but I could hardly tell her she was a wreck.

"I feel awful and I look worse," said Kate, aiming a tissue at the wastebasket. She missed.

She did look pretty bad. Her nose was still red, and her hair was almost as greasy as when she'd come home from Chicago. She had lost weight. There were gaunt hollows in her cheeks, and the expression on her face was full-blown grouch.

"You look awful for you, pretty good for me," I said.

"Oh, cut it out. I'm in no mood for it." Kate slid down under the covers, glaring at me and pouting out her lower lip.

"I'm tired of all this," she said sulkily. "I'm tired of being sick, and I'm tired of snow and of lying in bed all day staring out the window at that bare-naked tree and that ugly gray sky. Doesn't the sun ever shine in Ohio?''

"Occasionally," I said, as if admitting a tiny flaw in my favorite state. "Along about March or April, the clouds will break. We'll buy you a pair of sunglasses so the strain on your eyes isn't too great."

"By that time I'll be back in California," she said, but she didn't sound very excited about it. "I'll probably never see snow again, not unless I go looking for it."

"You can surf," I pointed out, "and pick oranges. And next year you can be with Jason at Berkeley."

"I'm not going to Berkeley," said Kate.

"You're not?"

"I'm going to nursing school in Whittier, the way I'd planned. Dating Jason isn't going to change that."

I was so surprised I didn't know what to say. To cover it, I scratched with my nails on Alfred's screen. He hissed obligingly.

I hissed back. "I never thought I could relate to a snake," I told Kate, "but I was wrong. Alfred's okay."

"He smells bad."

"You shouldn't say such things in front of him." I eyed Alfred more closely. If his feelings were hurt, he was doing an admirable job of hiding the fact.

"To tell the truth, I don't even *like* snakes," said Kate.

"Then why'd you bring him along?"

"I told you. Dad handed him to me at the airport. What else could I do, dump him in the nearest trash barrel?"

I didn't have an answer for that. "He does have a certain amount of charm," I told her.

"You like him?"

"Sure." What else could I say? Alfred was listening.

"Then he's yours."

"Mine?"

"I give him to you as a gift. I'll tell Dad you thought Alfred was charming, so I gave him to you. Dad will understand. He thinks snakes are pretty fascinating too."

"Thank you," I said. "I'm certain Alfred will make a great pet. He can't bark and has no claws to sharpen on the furniture. He doesn't even have to be taken for walks."

I looked back at Alfred. I think he had decided to take a nap, but I wasn't sure. It was hard to tell since he couldn't close his eyes. If he could have, he would have winked at me. After all, life was playing a big joke on me, Joni Allen. In the middle of my senior year, Kate had ended up with Jason, and I had ended up with a snake.

14

If it hadn't been for the National Honor Society assembly and Tomo, I might have proceeded through the next day with ease, handing in the Health papers and daydreaming about the weekend and my nearing freedom from Computers. But then, it wasn't all the fault of the assembly or of Tomo either. Part of my problem was that I'd turned off my alarm and gone back to sleep in the morning.

When Mom finally called me, I had to dash to the bathroom, throw on the clothes from the back of my desk chair, grab my books, and run. Then I charged back upstairs and into Kate's darkened bedroom. I grabbed her report, careened down the stairs, and out the door.

As it was, I barely made the bus. I ran down the sidewalk, screeching and waving one arm. When the driver saw me, she stopped the bus to let me on. Sinking breathless into the nearest empty seat, I thought my troubles were over.

To tell the truth, I'd forgotten about the Honor Society assembly. I suppose as vice president that

was careless of me, but really I had very little to do
with it. Tomo was president. He'd run the meeting
while Jason, Sue Christie, and I, the other officers,
sat on stage and tried to look intelligent. All I had to
do was report to the auditorium first period to help
set up the stage for the program.

It should have been easy, and it was. As we
arranged the lectern and carried chairs, we laughed
and talked about the students who were going to be
inducted, and recalled when we were chosen last
spring. Then Amy and Camilla Jones, who'd asked
for passes from their study hall, came to help us, and
we became silly. Tomo became silliest of all.

"My brother says you're in his karate class," said
Camilla.

"Which one's your brother?"

"He only started last week. He's a little kid, a
freshman. My dad thought karate might build his
self-confidence."

"It does," said Tomo seriously. "Until I took
karate, I was very short and shy."

"It made you grow?" asked Camilla.

"I stand taller because I know I can protect myself."

Amy snorted, then pressed one hand over her mouth,
trying not to laugh out loud.

"My brother wants to break boards with his hands,"
said Camilla, making a face. "I think that's stupid."

"It's all a matter of psyching yourself up," said
Tomo. "That and technique and strength. For ex-
ample—" His eyes searched the area of the stage,
across the dusty floor, around the heavy folds of red
curtain, beyond.

"I thought you had to build gradually to breaking
boards," said Jason. "Didn't you read that book the
instructor gave you?"

"I've read lots of books," said Tomo. "Ah, here

we are.'' He crossed the stage to pick up a board that had been shoved out of the way along one wall. He brought it back to us and laid it across the backs of two chairs.

''The bell's going to ring any minute,'' I said. The stage looked nice now. I didn't think its appearance would improve by being covered with splintered wood.

''Tomo, you've only been taking karate for—'' began Jason.

''Stand back,'' interrupted Tomo. ''Quiet. This is a matter of total concentration.''

He raised his right hand to shoulder height, held it perfectly straight, then brought it down swiftly across the board.

There was a clatter from the board, then a crash as one of the chairs fell over. Tomo didn't make a sound. He only stood there, staring at his hand. Then he grabbed a white T-shirt from the top of a pile of books near the lectern. He held it against his hand, pressing hard.

''Hey, that's my gym shirt,'' said Sue.

Tomo didn't answer, but then he didn't have to. We all saw the white shirt turn red. Blood began to drip on the stage floor.

''There must have been something sharp along the edge of the wood,'' said Amy.

''Come on, Tomo,'' said Jason. ''We'd better get you to the school nurse.''

''The assembly's in ten minutes,'' I said.

''Have the vice president take over,'' suggested Camilla.

''But I'm the vice president!'' I howled.

They all looked at me. Tomo said, very reasonably, ''Listen, I'll go to the nurse. If she can fix it, fine. If not, my notes are on the lectern. You'll have to chair the assembly. Bleeding on the inductees isn't part of the initiation."

What could I say? I stared down over the jumbled assortment of clothes I'd grabbed from the chair that morning, then went to look in my locker for something more suitable. There wasn't much, although I did find a pair of high heels shoved in the back behind some muddy boots. I borrowed a black blazer from Camilla, and was back onstage in time to glance at Tomo's notes before students began filing into the auditorium.

It could have been worse. Our adviser announced that Tomo was unable to be with us and that as vice president I was taking over on very short notice. I took a deep breath, had a couple of seconds' gratitude that Tomo had written very neat notes, and plunged in. Then I was too busy to worry about how I was doing.

Afterward everyone was very nice. They congratulated me and said I'd done a super job. Several teachers shook my hand. Jason told me the school nurse had run Tomo to the hospital for stitches, but that the cut wasn't as bad as we'd thought.

Somehow, as if awakening from a dream, I found myself once more in front of my locker, mechanically removing books and notebooks, kicking off the heels and slipping into low shoes, trying to remember which class I was to report to now.

It was Health. As I slid into my seat, I was congratulating myself. All I had to do was hand in our reports, and I could relax for the rest of the day. I shuffled through my notebook and pulled out my report on cancer. Then I began looking for the yellow folder that held Kate's report.

I couldn't find it. I went through all my notebooks and my stack of books, but it wasn't there.

By that time Mrs. Mastriani had come into the room and was rapping on the desk with a ruler for attention.

"People. Please be quiet, people," she said.

The boy behind me made a very rude noise. The rest of the students kept right on talking.

"People, please be seated and take out your research papers."

As the tardy bell rang, I searched frantically. I knew I had the report.

"Now people, pass your papers forward."

I calmed myself and tried to think what could have happened. I'd grabbed the report and shoved it in with my books as I ran for the bus. What happened afterward was a bit hazy, thanks to the assembly, but Kate's report had to be with the books I'd left in my locker. I raised my hand.

"Mrs. Mastriani, may I please go to my locker? I forgot the research paper."

"What do you have in your hand?"

"This is my paper. The one I forgot is my cousin's. She's home sick."

A few seconds passed on the clock next to the public address system. Then Mrs. Mastriani said, "You know I never permit any student to leave my room for any reason."

That was absolutely true. Maybe Mrs. Mastriani would let a student leave if they were having a heart attack or convulsions, or threw up. As far as I knew, it hadn't happened yet.

"Aargh," I said, bending over and clutching my stomach. "I have the most horrible pain!"

"Miss Allen, if you really are ill, I will give you a pass to the nurse's office, but you may not return to my class today." As I straightened in my seat, she added, "However, since forgetting the paper was an error on your part, it would be unjust to punish your cousin for it. Therefore, I will permit you to bring the paper to this room and place it on my desk after school.''

There was applause from the freshmen and scattered moans of delight at her generosity.

''I will point out that I'll not be here because I must leave for an appointment with my orthodontist. However, the room will be open for cleaning. I'll collect the paper before school Monday morning.''

Mrs. Mastriani bared her braces at us. ''That will be enough, people. Pass your papers forward.''

I passed in my paper, telling myself that everything was all right, that Kate's paper was in my locker; but I didn't really believe it, not until I opened my locker that afternoon and found the paper in a stack of books. I raced upstairs to the room where Mrs. Mastriani taught.

She wasn't there. A man with a very round middle and a very small head was mopping the floor by her desk as if he expected the job to last well into the night. When I came into the room, he stopped mopping and sighed loudly. His gray eyes, swimming in his soft white face, reminded me of raw oysters.

''What do you want, girlie?'' he asked. He was chewing on a toothpick, rolling it from one corner of his mouth to the other.

''I brought this paper in for Mrs. Mastriani.''

''She ain't here.''

''I know. I'm supposed to leave it on her desk.''

''All right by me.'' He shrugged, the oyster eyes never leaving me for a second.

I put the research paper on the desk. *HEALTH* glowed up in blue ink through the yellow transparent cover. Kate's name was in the upper right corner, the class period beneath it. I frowned, reaching for the paper. It seemed strange that Kate hadn't written *The Respiratory System* on the cover page.

"You want something else?" asked the man. He gave a sort of grunt and moved closer, his left arm brushing my right one.

"No," I muttered, "thank you." And I fled.

15

Kate seemed to feel a lot better over the weekend. At least she dressed and came to meals. But she was terribly quiet, even for Kate. If I hadn't known better, I'd have thought she was avoiding me. She was short with Jason when he called after lunch Sunday. I heard her tell him she didn't want to see him that evening, that she would catch him in school Monday. Then she went to her room.

Mother told me to leave her alone, but I couldn't. There was something wrong with Kate, more than the flu, and I was afraid it might have to do with me. I gave her a few minutes, then followed her upstairs.

The door to Kate's room was closed. I waited outside, listening. She could have been taking a nap. When I heard a shifting sound on the bed, I rapped on the door.

There was a muffled reply from inside. I opened the door and looked in.

Kate was sitting in bed, fully dressed, wearing the green sweater I'd given her for Christmas. She was propped against her pillows with a blanket pulled over her legs. On the blanket were a box of tissues, a letter from Africa, a stack of books and notebooks, and the small stuffed toy mouse that one of her friends from Oakland had sent her for Christmas.

Kate was still pale and drawn-looking, with circles under her eyes, but she had washed her hair. It lay soft and shining, curling gently to her shoulders.

"Can I come in?" I asked.

"I don't care."

I entered the room, stood at the foot of the bed, then went to the window. Kate wasn't saying anything encouraging; so I took refuge in her desk chair, my right arm lying on the desk next to Alfred's aquarium, which I planned to move to my room as soon as I'd cleared a spot for it.

"The kids have been asking about you," I told her. "Some of the kids" would be more truthful, but they were asking. Tomo had sent a card, and so had Amy.

Kate didn't answer. She picked up the stuffed mouse and twisted its tail around one index finger.

"Is something wrong?" I asked.

"What could possibly be wrong?"

"I don't know. You're acting funny."

She moved her legs restlessly under the covers. "Maybe I'm a funny person."

"Are you mad at me?"

Kate looked directly at me. She sighed. "No," she said. "Actually, I'm mad at my father."

"Why?"

"Because he went to Africa!" Her fingers clutched at the mouse. She eyed it, then threw it in a weary gesture toward the stack of books. "I don't see how he could do that to me."

"It's his job."

"My senior year in high school? He wrecked my

whole year. He's always going off somewhere to look at snakes. He doesn't care anything about me.''

"He didn't have a choice," I pointed out. "The government sent him.''

"Yeah," said Kate. "I wish the government would mind its own business and stop messing around in my life.''

"He'll be home soon. It's only eight more weeks.''

"A lot of good that'll do me.'' She reached out one slender arm and picked up the letter from Africa. "Listen to this.'' She searched the pages and read, 'We've had the greatest piece of good luck, Kate. The people who are renting our house in Oakland want to buy it. I'll be free to rent an apartment near the university, which will be a lot smaller, much better for me with you away in nursing school next year. I'm sorry this means you won't be able to finish school in Oakland. But it's only three months, and I'm certain the high school in Berkeley is excellent—' '' Her voice broke off, and she started to cry, dropping the letter and fumbling at the box of tissues.

"Oh, Kate," I said. "That's awful. How can he be so mean?''

"He's not mean," said Kate, crying into the tissue. "He just doesn't understand. He goes around all the time studying his snakes, and he doesn't really understand that I don't have a wonderful time too.''

"But what will you do?''

"Go to Berkeley High," she said, rubbing fiercely at her cheeks, scrubbing away the tears.

"You can stay here," I offered.

"You're joking.'' She tilted her head at me, disbelief narrowing her eyes.

"No, I'm not. I'm sure it would be okay with Mom and Dad.''

"I thought you hated me."

"I don't hate you," I said. "I like you." I shifted uneasily. "Maybe I was put off by you at first. You weren't what I expected. You weren't like all the kids I'm used to."

"Like what?"

"You were so attractive—so tall and elegant and sophisticated. You looked as if you spent every day of your life hopping in and out of planes, going to exotic places."

"I was scared," said Kate. "I couldn't remember ever meeting any of you people. Then you kept calling me Kathy. I hate that name. That's what Icky Arnie always calls me."

"You were wearing that expensive blazer and skirt, and all your luggage matched," I said.

"You looked so chic," said Kate.

"Me? Chic? In my brother's old raincoat?"

"Like one of those girls in the fashion magazines who can wear anything and get away with it. I think it's the air of confidence that carries it off."

Boy, had Kate got it wrong. I hastened to set her straight. "I'm not confident," I said. "I'm klutzy. Good-hearted, but klutzy."

"And brilliant. That's what my dad always says about you. Lois's girl, Joni, is brilliant. And you are. I found that out."

"Hey. Look at Computers."

"Computers." She dismissed the curse of my life with a wave of one hand. "You have it all together. You don't have to work for your friends. Everything comes easy to you."

"You think that?" I asked in amazement.

"Everything in your whole life is worked out, all very neatly. I never know what's going to happen to me, but you're so certain of everything."

I couldn't believe I was hearing right. Nothing was certain for me anymore, not Jason, not my future, not anything. I looked at Kate. She fell silent for a moment, tearing a clean tissue into shreds. From her point of view, I was the lucky one. Why had I thought we had to be rivals?

Kate began talking again, but I was thinking instead of listening. The girl on the bed was not the same girl who had stepped off the plane in October. She was more relaxed, not so cool and aloof anymore. She also seemed more genuine.

"Of course I've had boyfriends," Kate was saying, "since elementary school. But not the way you girls do here."

"What do you mean?"

"The girls in your gang seem tight with their guys, you know? It's as if they're all headed for forever and ever."

Was it that way? I shifted uncomfortably, thinking of Jennifer and Sam, of Jason and me before we broke up.

"Even the kids who are going to college don't plan on changing anything," continued Kate. "Not ever."

"Maybe that's a mistake."

"Hey. I didn't mean to take Jason away from you. We were only friends. It just happened."

"I don't think you did take him," I said slowly. "We probably would have broken up anyway, sooner or later."

Kate plucked at the edge of her blanket, then with a kick of one foot threw it off. "Anyway," she said with a sigh, "I'm stuck with another new school and another new set of kids to deal with." She reached forward, tugging at the blanket, pulling it back up over her legs.

Kate pulled too hard. The box of tissues, stuffed mouse, and letter from Africa went flying as the blanket came free from the bottom of the bed.

I jumped to my feet and grabbed, but I was too late. Her stack of books and notebooks tumbled to the floor with the rest.

"I'll get them," I offered, kneeling to shuffle papers together and pick up books. I hesitated, a yellow folder in one hand.

"What's that?" asked Kate, leaning over the side of the bed to see.

"I don't know." The bright yellow cover was transparent. Through it, the cover page showed clearly. *The Respiratory System* was written neatly in black.

"But I turned this in," I said, staring at the report in horror. "I know I did. I made a special trip after school because I forgot and left it in my locker."

I glanced from the paper up into Kate's green eyes. We froze motionless for several seconds.

"Oh, no," I groaned, sinking back onto my heels. "I turned in your story about Mrs. Mastriani corrupting the elementary school kids."

Kate made a little choking sound, then threw herself back on her pillows. "That's it. I'm not going to graduate at all. Not anywhere."

"Oh, Kate, I'm so sorry."

"I blew it," she said. "First I failed Health at home because I refused to do mouth-to-mouth resuscitation on a dummy after Icky Arnie. Now I write a dumb story about the teacher and turn it in instead of my term paper."

"You didn't turn it in," I pointed out. "I did."

"Thanks a lot," she said bitterly. "I'm so glad you helped."

"I said I'm sorry." I pushed down the unreasonable hostility that arose at her anger. Kate had a right to be mad at me. How could I do such a stupid thing? I took her report and put it on her desk next to Alfred's aquarium.

Kate mumbled something else.

I turned and asked, "What?"

"Nothing," she muttered, frowning. Then she looked depressed. "Forget it."

"I can't forget it." I threw one arm wide, my hand hitting Alfred's tank, knocking the screen on top askew. Alfred vibrated his tail, but otherwise did nothing.

"Maybe I could go to school early tomorrow and substitute this paper for the other one before she sees it," said Kate. Her eyes were so shiny I was afraid she might cry.

"Mrs. Mastriani has to unlock the room," I told her. "She'll notice the report on her desk, and she'll never let you switch without checking it first."

We were both silent for a moment. Then Kate said, "I wonder if they have Health in summer school in Berkeley." She looked as pale and tired as she had when she was coming down with the flu.

Feeling numb, I picked up the screen to Alfred's tank and leaned over to replace it. The rock balanced perilously and almost fell inside.

Alfred raised the front part of his body and puffed himself up, looking impressive.

"Don't give up yet," I told Kate, staring at Alfred. "I've just had a great idea."

16

Are you sure this is a great idea?'' asked Kate. Dad had dropped us off early at school on his way to work. In the car Kate had seemed confident; but now, carrying Alfred's traveling box in one hand and her stack of books in the other, she was having doubts.

"Of course." I ran across the parking lot toward the building. The temperature stood at 15 that morning. I didn't want Alfred to go into hibernation and ruin everything.

"Wait," said Kate, puffing after me into the building. "I don't want to get suspended."

"That can't be any worse than failing Health. You can get suspended and still graduate. Did Alfred go into hibernation?"

"In thirty seconds?" Kate raised the box to eye level and tried to peer into one of the air holes. "No. I can't see him, but I can hear him moving around."

"Remember. If anyone asks what we're doing in the building twenty minutes early and equipped with a snake, Mrs. Kollas asked to borrow him for Biology.''

"Did she?''

"No, Kate," I explained patiently. "I told you all that. My freshman year, Mrs. Kollas mentioned she'd like to have a snake to show us, and I just remembered in time for her to show her classes this year.''

When Kate looked doubtful, I said, "Give Alfred to me." I shifted my books to my right arm, undid one of the latches on the box, and carried it in my left hand. "You have your paper ready?''

"Right inside the cover of my notebook.''

"Let's go.''

I thought we had plenty of time, but when we rounded the corner of the corridor, I could see a light on in Mrs. Mastriani's room. The door stood open.

"I've flunked," said Kate under her breath.

"Hurry!" My hands were sweating. I gripped the handle of the box more securely and practically ran.

Mrs. Mastriani was standing at the door to her closet, hanging up her coat. She turned to look at us as we entered the room.

"Hello, people," she said, reaching down and stripping off a boot, putting it in the closet, and sliding her foot into one of the shoes she had placed on the floor. "What can I do for you?''

"We got here early," I mumbled, moving nearer her desk.

"I can see that." Mrs. Mastriani took off her second boot, put it in the closet, and fumbled with her foot at her other shoe. "What do you want?''

"I wondered if you graded the research papers yet," I said.

"Most of them." She slammed the closet door and came to join us.

Kate edged closer to the desk, looked at me, and bit her lower lip.

"I see your cousin is with you," said Mrs. Mastriani. "I trust you have fully recovered." She didn't sound very fond of Kate.

"Yes, Mrs. Mastriani," said Kate. Her voice was high and thin, and sounded nervous.

"And here is your paper which Joni turned in Friday," said Mrs. Mastriani. "I'll put it with the others." She reached for it.

Time for Alfred to spring into action. In one swift motion, I put his box on the desk, flipped up the second latch, and spilled him out.

"Oh!" I screamed. "The box came open! He escaped!"

Kate had told me that snakes can't move on smooth surfaces. Mrs. Mastriani's desk top must not be smooth. Alfred crossed the desk like lightning.

"What's that?" demanded Mrs. Mastriani.

"A snake!" screamed Kate. "An escaped snake!"

I think she overdid it. Mrs. Mastriani glanced at her and frowned suspiciously. "This wouldn't have anything to do with your paper, would it?" she asked, reaching once more for it.

Alfred was magnificent. When Mrs. Mastriani's hand approached the desk, he went into his act. He hissed, shook his tail violently, and raised the front portion of his body.

Mrs. Mastriani froze.

Alfred began to puff himself up, still hissing. Then he struck.

"Ahh!" shrieked Mrs. Mastriani, jerking her hand.

Poor Alfred was so frightened that he threw himself on his back and played dead.

"Get him!" yelled Mrs. Mastriani.

I sagged, holding on to one corner of the desk and pretending to faint.

Kate widened her eyes and made her mouth into a big circle until she looked like someone in a silent horror film.

"Get help," she squeaked, trying to sound breathless.

"You go," said Mrs. Mastriani.

"I can't move," whispered Kate slowly, dramatically. "I think he bit me."

Mrs. Mastriani glanced at me. I closed my eyes tightly and moaned, then slitted them to keep a check on the situation.

Alfred had recovered enough to begin to turn onto his stomach.

That was too much for Mrs. Mastriani. She ran out of the room and down the hall. We could hear her heels clattering on the terrazzo floor.

"Quick," hissed Kate.

I opened my eyes fully to see her take the paper labeled *HEALTH* from the desk and shove it into the notebook on the bottom of her stack of books. Then she removed her research paper from the top notebook and placed it on the desk.

I grabbed Alfred firmly behind his head and lifted him, supporting his long body with my left hand.

We could hear Mrs. Mastriani returning, her voice shrill, talking to someone she had with her.

Kate held the box open, and I lowered Alfred inside. Kate was closing the latches when Mrs. Mastriani burst into the room.

She had the fat janitor with the oyster eyes with her. He carried a tire iron in one hand and a chain in the other. I guess he intended to club Alfred to death with the tire iron. I don't know what he meant to do with the chain.

"Stand back, everybody," he said, raising the tire iron and advancing on the desk. "I'll handle this."

"It's okay," said Kate. "We got him back into his box."

"Are you sure?" asked Mrs. Mastriani.

"Yes." I held it up. "Want to look?"

"No, thank you." She puffed out her cheeks and let out a big sigh of air, then gave a tired smile to the janitor. I noticed that she'd had her braces removed over the weekend. It didn't improve her appearance much.

Then Mrs. Mastriani remembered she was the teacher and we were the students. "What are you doing with that creature in this school?" she demanded.

"We're lending him to Mrs. Kollas to show her Biology class," I told her.

"Where'd you get it?"

"From my father," said Kate. "He's a herpetologist."

As we left the room, Mrs. Mastriani followed us to the door. She stood there watching suspiciously as we went down the hall and turned into Mrs. Kollas's room.

Mrs. Kollas seemed confused by Alfred. She said she couldn't remember having requested a snake for her classes, but now that he was here she supposed it was a good idea. She placed a clean aquarium on a lab table, then looked around, trying to locate a cover for it.

"I don't seem to have a screen," she said. "I must have lent it to another teacher. You want to put him in the aquarium?"

As Kate took Alfred from his box and lowered him into his temporary home, it occurred to me that Alfred had seen more action in the last hour than he had in months.

"He's a beauty," said Mrs. Kollas, watching Alfred coil neatly behind the glass. "What kind of snake is he?"

"A hog-nosed snake," I told her. "See? He has a little snout on the end of his nose."

"Really fine," she said. "You girls wait here with him while I go down to the science supply room for another screen."

When Mrs. Kollas had left the room, Kate's eyes met mine over the lab table.

"Stand back, everybody," I ordered in a low voice. "I'll handle this."

Kate started to giggle. Then she laughed out loud. "It worked," she said. "It really worked. I thought by now we'd be sitting in the principal's office, trying to explain my story about Mrs. Mastriani and what we were doing with Alfred in school."

"I told you it was a great idea," I said modestly.

17

The Friday of exam week, we have no school. That is traditional in our town. I think the school board hopes that in three days we'll refresh our brains for another big round of education.

Once again Steve and I had planned a ski trip. In preparation, he'd come over to my house twice, bringing his boots, skis, and poles. He'd placed me on the skis, explaining how to stop by sinking down, shifting my knees, and pressing on the inner sides of my feet. I stood in our backyard in the dirty, half-melting remains of snow and tried to pretend I was somewhere in the Alps preparing for the winter Olympics.

It didn't work. Even without moving, I could barely stay upright. "I'll probably end up with a broken leg," I predicted.

"Trust me. You'll be terrific."

I shot Steve a look, thinking how much I liked that deep voice of his. "Do they have beginners' slopes?"

"Sure. Now concentrate. Shifting your weight is very important."

I concentrated, but I didn't get to use what I

learned Friday. By Thursday of exam week, we had snow. It began as tiny sparkles of ice in the early morning air, then grew into large, soft flakes as the day wore on. By last period there was some question as to how buses carrying students to the outlying districts would get through. We had four inches of the white stuff on the ground, and more came piling out of the sky in an endless supply.

When my alarm went off at six Friday morning, I rolled over, shut it off, and lay for a minute wondering what I was doing awake on a vacation day. Then I jumped out of bed and ran to the window.

All the world was white. A few stray flakes drifted earthward across what seemed to be a sea of snow. Far off, I heard the rumble of a snowplow. Perfect skiing weather. Or was it?

I dressed in thermal underwear, corduroy pants, a blouse, heavy sweater, and boots. Then I gathered my scarf and jacket and mittens, my hat and an extra sweater, and went downstairs.

At six thirty I was sipping hot tea at the kitchen table, blowing the steam away from my face and wondering if I should shed my sweater. It was cold outside, but it was warm and cozy in the kitchen. I was also debating whether to call Steve when the phone rang.

"Did you look outside?" he asked.

"Perfect skiing weather."

There was a little silence. Then Steve said, "What about driving weather?"

"Oh, Steve!"

"All the minor highways are closed, and there are travel restrictions on 177."

"Are you sure?"

"I called the traffic patrol."

"Terrific." I chewed at my bottom lip.

There was nothing to do but go back to bed. I left my clothes in a crumpled heap on the floor and dived in, curling into a ball in the sudden cold of the sheets.

When I awoke again, it was almost noon, and the snow had stopped completely. Kate and I made grilled cheese sandwiches for lunch, then spent the afternoon cutting big letters out of poster board for my mother.

"What's she want these for?" asked Kate, eyeing a blister from the scissors on her right hand.

"It's some idea she has to lure her first graders into reading. Each kid has a letter; then they get together in groups and form words."

"Sort of a primitive Group 4."

"Sort of," I agreed sourly.

"Hey, it's not the end of the world because you didn't go skiing."

"I know. I'm just grumpy. I'm bored."

"Me too." She picked at the blister. "Want to make a snowman?"

"It's not the right kind of snow."

Kate raised an eyebrow.

"It's not packing snow," I explained. "You have to have packing snow for a snowman."

Kate sighed. Then she said, "It's pretty."

"Pretty deep."

At four, I called Steve back figuring he wasn't going anywhere.

"I have an idea," I said. "Why don't we go sledding in the park this evening? I'll call Amy. She has two little brothers, and they're bound to have sleds."

"I have a toboggan."

"You're kidding."

"I spent the last hour waxing the bottom."

"I'll call Amy anyway. We can get a bunch of kids together and make it a sledding party."

"I'll pick you up at seven."

"Make it eight. Some of the kids eat late."

By eight, it was snowing again, but not seriously. Soft, furry flakes fell from the sky, more like those on television than for real. Steve drove up in his parents' old green Rabbit, his toboggan fastened on the roof, and Kate and I ran out and piled in.

"I got everybody but Jason," I told Steve. "I tried to reach him before dinner, and Kate called after, but his phone line must be down."

Steve shrugged, then concentrated on driving until we reached the street leading to the park. We left the car there, not wanting to risk the hills and curves inside the park.

Amy and Tomo were sitting on a bench by the lake, staring at the frozen water. Amy looked like one of Santa's elves, dressed in green with a matching stocking hat. Tomo had on a heavy red jacket and thick mittens, but he wore no cap. A dusting of snow frosted his black curls.

"Miranda and Harry went up to the big hill by the tennis courts, explained Amy. "So did Jennifer and Sam. We told them we'd wait for you here."

"Thanks. What's that?" I asked.

"My snow disk," said Tomo. He knocked the snow from the disk. "Let's go. I can't wait to try the toboggan."

The hills at the park must have been crowded all day with kids, but by that time of evening they were practically deserted. We went beyond the tennis courts to find an empty slope of deep soft snow against a background of spruce trees.

I wasn't glad Steve and I'd missed our skiing trip, but I don't see how it could have been any better than an evening in the snow. When finally the snow stopped falling, the wind picked up, but exercise and being piled on the toboggan with other kids kept me warm. Although we took turns, we sent Kate on most of the rides. I guess all of us wanted to show her that winter wasn't only gray skies and naked trees. In many ways, it was one of the best seasons of the year.

Jennifer and Sam had already gone home when Tomo and Amy, Harry and Miranda, and Kate made the last run about midnight. The toboggan started slow under their weight, then picked up speed when Steve gave a hard shove on Harry's back.

I shivered and clapped my hands. Steve circled me with his arms to hug me away from the wind, then leaned over and picked up Tomo's disk, abandoned in the snow.

"Let's try this," he suggested, dumping the snow off it.

"Will we fit?"

"Like pieces in a puzzle."

Tight, he meant. Somehow we did manage to get on, me in front, Steve behind, his legs wrapped around me, his gloved hands clutching the hand holds on the side of the disk. We wiggled the disk into motion and were suddenly flying down the run.

The disk ran faster than the toboggan, its smooth bottom skimming over the path. Not only was it fast, it twirled as we went, like a merry-go-round gone crazy. I screamed and grabbed at the sides. Round and round we went, ever faster, flying by the stand of spruce trees dark against the sky, past a little frozen pond on a flat place, on past Harry and Miranda, Tomo and Amy, and Kate, who were stopped at the bottom of the slope.

The disk hit the huge mound of snow past the bottom of the toboggan run, slid up it, and poised for a second at the very top, then tilted over and dumped us on the other side.

I landed on my back, my breath knocked from me in a gasp. I choked, then pulled air deep into my lungs, so deep that the cold icy night seemed to enter and fill me, hurting in its intensity.

Steve had landed a few feet away on his stomach. I turned my head toward him as he crawled to me on his elbows.

"You okay?"

I nodded, glancing at him, then beyond. The sky above us was black, a sprinkle of stars in it, twinkling silver against velvet. Then it was almost as if I could see myself lying in the snow, the snowflakes on me a sprinkle of white like the stars.

I stared up at Steve. His eyes were huge; his knitted cap covered with snow. He leaned over, kissed me, and said, "You're my girl."

I smiled but I didn't answer, because I was nobody's girl. For the first time ever, I was free. And I felt the way I had on the toboggan, as if I were spinning round and round, flying free, free to be my own self—Joni—at last, to discover the person who was me.

18

That was January. This is June. I still have Alfred, but Kate doesn't have Jason anymore. Jason has been dating Marcy since February, and Kate is going to the senior party with Scott Miller. I'm still dating Steve; but sometimes when Jason's and my eyes meet, I shiver inside and wonder if I do love him.

After school this afternoon, Kate came into my room without knocking. She was carrying a letter from her father which had arrived in the morning's mail.

"Listen to this," she said, flopping down onto the jumble of blankets and pillows and clothes that covered my bed. "My dad says, 'I've thought a lot about it, and I've decided that I am definitely coming east to your graduation. That's one event I don't want to miss, especially since I came home in March by way of Hawaii and didn't see you then. I miss you, Kate, more than I realized I would, and soon you'll be grown up and gone.'"

"You're grown up and gone now," I said, but Kate ignored the interruption.

" 'I'll call your aunt on the fifth to tell her when to expect me, but I wanted you to be the first to know.' " She lowered the page. "He's coming."

"That's terrific."

"Whoopee!" Kate bounded off the bed. She leaned over and made kissing sounds at Alfred, then straightened and turned toward the door.

"I'm going to tell Aunt Lois," she said, reaching to brush away a piece of hair that had strayed across her right cheek.

The gesture brought back with incredible clarity that early morning after the Homecoming Dance, when I'd stood behind the plate-glass window at the airport and seen my cousin for the first time. While she was talking to the college boy, she'd reached, exactly like that, to brush a piece of hair from her cheek.

What a long time ago that seems, I thought to myself as Kate left the room, and what a short time it was. I began to pick up clothes from the bed, sorting the clean ones to put in my dresser. I am trying to become neater, because I might have a roommate in the fall at Case Western.

I put a pink nightie into my middle drawer, shifting other clothes to make room. The music box and Jason's Christmas present were in that drawer. I hadn't looked at them in months. I opened the small velvet box and took out the rings.

They lay, two gold circles, on the palm of my left hand. I picked them up and tried to place them together, the way they had been when I first saw them.

They slipped together easily and became one. I stared at them, thinking of Jason and me, and moved my fingers. The rings came apart again, each a complete individual circle.

Would Jason and I go together again like the rings? I didn't know. I put them away and reached for the music box, eyeing the two small figures on top of it.

Some of the gilt was gone from the girl's dress, and both the boy and the girl were dusty. I touched them gently. Then I wound the golden key and listened to the tinkle of the notes, watching the figures spin, the girl with her frozen smile turning rigidly to the sounds of the box.

I raised my eyes from the tiny figure to look in the mirror. The girl staring back at me looked very much as she had last October: dark hair, dark eyes, a hint of laughter around the wide mouth. She looked the same, but she was not. At Homecoming I'd been like the girl on top of the music box, rigid and formed. Everything was set and settled, and I thought I could be happy that way forever.

Life on the music box where there's no room to grow, I thought as I put it away with the rings in my drawer. Suddenly I smiled at the girl in the mirror. Then slowly, thoughtfully, I began to sway. Humming a melody, I moved, creating my own original dance.

NANCY J. HOPPER, a former high school English teacher, began writing professionally while raising her two children. Since 1979, she has written seven other books for children and young adults.

"I like to have a blend of seriousness and humor in my books," she says, "because I believe that life itself is an awesome blend of the serious and the comic."

RIVALS, like her earlier stories, is based partly on her experiences while growing up in central Pennsylvania. She now lives in Alliance, Ohio, with her husband, a college art professor.

AVON FLARE BESTSELLERS

by BRUCE AND CAROLE HART

SOONER OR LATER   42978-0/$2.95US/$3.75Can
Thirteen-year-old Jessie is a romantic and ready for her first love. She knows that if she's patient, the *real* thing is bound to happen. And it does, with Michael—handsome, charming and seventeen!

WAITING GAMES   79012-2/$2.95US/$3.75Can
Michael and Jessie's story continues as they learn what being in love really means. How much are they willing to share together—if their love is to last forever?

BREAKING UP IS HARD TO DO
                    89970-1/$3.50US/$3.95Can
Julie and Sean don't know each other, but they have one big thing in common—they both are falling in love for the first time...and they're about to learn there's a world of difference between first love and lasting love.

and a new romance

CROSS YOUR HEART   89971-X/$2.95US/$3.95Can
Ignoring her friends' warnings, Angelica falls for Gary —the gorgeous new senior with a mysterious past— until she is forced to face the truth.